"T‍here's not even an ex—Mrs. Gant?"

"No."

"How about a significant other?"

"No."

"Of either gender?"

He smiled. "No. And just for the record I'm extremely and exclusively heterosexual."

"That's good. That's very good." Mischievous laughter lit her eyes. "Wow! Imagine the women of San Francisco letting you run free all these years! There must be something seriously wrong with the water supply that's impaired their good sense."

He couldn't help it. He had to laugh. "Are you always this direct?"

"Yes. Does it make you uncomfortable?"

"No. Just disarmed."

She grinned. "That's good. I like a man who is without weapons."

WHAT ARE *LOVESWEPT* ROMANCES?

They are stories of true romance and touching emotion. We believe those two very important ingredients are constants in our highly sensual and very believable stories in the LOVESWEPT *line. Our goal is to give you, the reader, stories of consistently high quality that may sometimes make you laugh, sometimes make you cry, but are always fresh and creative and contain many delightful surprises within their pages.*

Most romance fans read an enormous number of books. Those they truly love, they keep. Others may be traded with friends and soon forgotten. We hope that each LOVESWEPT *romance will be a treasure—a "keeper." We will always try to publish*

LOVE STORIES YOU'LL NEVER FORGET
BY AUTHORS YOU'LL ALWAYS REMEMBER

The Editors

LADY
BEWARE

FAYRENE
PRESTON

BANTAM BOOKS
NEW YORK · TORONTO · LONDON · SYDNEY · AUCKLAND

LADY BEWARE

A Bantam Book / June 1995

If you would be interested in receiving protective vinyl covers for your Loveswept books, please write to this address for information:

> *Loveswept*
> *Bantam Books*
> *P.O. Box 985*
> *Hicksville, NY 11802*

ISBN 0-553-44512-X

Published simultaneously in the United States and Canada

Bantam Books are published by Bantam Books, a division of Bantam Doubleday Dell Publishing Group, Inc. Its trademark, consisting of the words "Bantam Books" and the portrayal of a rooster, is Registered in U.S. Patent and Trademark Office and in other countries. Marca Registrada. Bantam Books, 1540 Broadway, New York, New York 10036.

PRINTED IN THE UNITED STATES OF AMERICA

OPM   0 9 8 7 6 5 4 3 2 1

ONE

"Where the hell did I put my keys?" Kendall muttered. With her knee propped against the outside hall of the apartment and a sack of groceries balanced precariously on her knee, she dug through her purse. "Like I'm in the mood for this now. Yeah, right." She blew a curly wisp of hair off her forehead just as her hand closed around a thin oblong object. Identifying it as a half-flattened candy bar, she tossed it back into the depths of her purse and continued searching. "Drat! They're in here. I know they're in here. They've *got* to be in here. On second thought, no, they don't have to be in here. They—"

"Excuse me, may I help?"

She started at the politely spoken question, then glanced around to see a man standing in front of the apartment next door, a set of keys and a bundle of mail in his hands. Her breath caught in her throat. She *knew* him. Or did she? No . . .

"What?" She was bewildered by the instantaneous feeling that she knew him, but at the same time was positive she didn't.

"You seem to be in a crisis situation and I asked if I could help you."

She stared at him, taking in the slant of his broad shoulders, the dark beige hue of his skin, and the warm brown color of his hair. He seemed incredibly familiar to her, yet as far as she was aware, she didn't know anyone in San Francisco.

And she knew for a fact that she had never looked into his eyes before. They were extraordinary, so deep a blue they might be mistaken for black from a distance.

She straightened away from the wall. "Excuse me, but have we met before?"

He returned her gaze with no sign of recognition. "I'm sure I would have remembered."

"Yes, I guess so." What he said made sense. Surely she would recall meeting a man like him. What woman wouldn't? He was six feet tall, slim, with dark, good looks that were more interesting than dazzling. In fact, there was nothing obvious about him. The unmistakable power of his body was subdued.

His posture was relaxed, assured. He didn't overpower. Instead he made a person want to stay awhile and perhaps draw closer. He also made everything sexual in her come alive, so alive, in fact, she was having to scramble to deal with it.

And somehow, in some way, in some part of her, she *did* know him. But how could that be?

"Are you sure we've never met before? I've only been here one other time about a year ago, but—"

He closed the distance between them and held out his hand. "I'm Steven Gant. I live next door."

His voice was deep and slightly husky and completely unfamiliar. She shifted the bag of groceries and her purse and held out her hand. "Hi, I'm Kendall Merrick." His hand closed around hers, firm and warm and comforting with its strength. An image, a feeling, flickered through her mind, tickling her memory, and then was gone before she could grasp it.

He dropped her hand and smiled. "Do you always talk to yourself?"

His smile stunned her. It involved his whole face and she felt its effects in the lower regions of her body as heat melted through her. "I'm sorry. What did you say?"

"I asked if you always talk to yourself."

"Only when there's no one else around to talk to."

"Then I guess it's a good thing I came along when I did. Now you'll have someone to talk to, plus you look like you could use some help."

"Help?" Boy, that was the truth. She definitely needed someone to bring her to her senses. Unfortunately she had no one but herself. "Oh . . . no, thanks . . . I'm just searching for my keys. But, listen, if by any chance your plans include participating in a scavenger hunt anytime soon, choose me for your team. I'll probably have all the items on the list in my purse. With the exception, of course, of the keys to this apartment." If she didn't know him, she reflected curiously, why was her heart beating so fast and all her nerve endings tingling? It was as if she knew his warmth, even his smell, without once having ever been close to him.

He smiled again. "Thanks for the tip. I'll remember that." He shifted his stance and glanced over his shoulder, and something in the movement triggered a memory.

Was it possible that this was the man who had been in her dreams lately? No, it couldn't be. It was ridiculous even to think it. To make it even more ridiculous the dreams she had been having were *erotic* dreams. Her skin flushed as she tried to talk herself out of the idea. She had never seen the face of the man in her dreams, so therefore . . . Lord help her, she'd bet money that the man standing before her was the same man she had been dreaming about for the last month. She swallowed hard.

"Are you all right?" he asked, watching her closely.

She smiled brightly, praying she wouldn't give herself away. "Oh, fine—just fine." How in the hell had he ended up in her dreams? And how could she explain the timing? Her dreams had started only about a month before. She'd chalked it up to her unsettled state after Reed's death and to the fact that she had felt so all alone. In the daylight, she had reasoned that she wanted comfort and so she had conjured up a dream lover. Weird, yes, but a totally innocuous act. And she had certainly done stranger things in her life.

Her heart lurched as her gaze fixed on his lips. Did she really know how his lips felt on hers? No. She knew how the man in her dreams had kissed. Magnificently. But then it would have been stupid of her to conjure up someone who hadn't. What would have been the point? If she was going to dream, her motto was dream the very best.

She looked at his hands and remembered that her dream lover had stroked her naked body in a way that had brought her awake night after night, aching with frustration. She had to be wrong about this man being in her dreams. She *had* to be. Her dream lover wasn't this man. They just *resembled* each other.

"Are you sure you're okay?"

She laughed. "Please don't worry about me. I'm just normally a little strange."

He smiled. "I find that hard to believe."

"Well, don't, because it's true." His face fascinated her. Strong-featured, with a firm jawline, his face was etched with weariness, as if he had seen a great deal of life and hadn't particularly cared for what he had seen. She shook her head, exasperated with herself. Her imagination was really out of control. "I'm sorry to keep staring at you, it's just that I can't shake the feeling that I know you somehow." He seemed to tense, but she had to be imagining that too. She had imagined a lot in the last six weeks. She had always had an active imagination, but by wishing this man to life, she'd really outdone herself.

Smiling to herself, she went back to fishing through her purse, letting her fingers identify by feel the assortment of objects. Lipstick. Compact. The candy bar again. A comb. Several old movie stubs. "How things can just disappear in my purse is a mystery to me. I swear to you, if scientists want to study black holes, they don't have to look any farther." She pulled up a mini-flashlight, glanced at it, then dropped it back into the purse.

He nodded toward the door behind her. "Are you moving in?"

Like a cold wash of reality the question brought her out of the befuddled state into which she had fallen when she had turned around and seen him. She sighed. "Not exactly. I'll only be here a short while to go through my brother's things and decide what I want to do with everything."

"You're Reed Jackson's sister?"

"Stepsister, actually," she said. Compassion crossed his face, bringing an even more interesting depth to his features. "His father married my mother when I was nine and Reed was fifteen."

"I was very sorry to hear of his death."

"Thank you. It was quite a shock." That was an understatement. Reed had died one rainy night six weeks ago when his car had slammed into a telephone pole. There had been no other car involved and his alcohol blood level had been normal. She had had Reed's body brought to San Luis Obispo, where she had lived all her life, and buried him in the same plot with his father and her mother and father.

A ghost of a smile touched her lips. She

liked to think of them as one big happy family in death as they had been in life. Theirs had been an extended family that had worked. Reed's death had left a hole in a corner of her life, but she had gone through her grieving process and now all that was left was for her to decide what to do with Reed's possessions.

"Did you know Reed?" she asked curiously.

He nodded. "I knew him, but not well. For instance I didn't know his father was still living."

"He's not. He and my mother were killed in an accident a few years ago." Her tone turned contemplative. "You'd think I'd get used to losing people I love in accidents but each time it has happened it has laid me out flat."

His face softened. "It would be unnatural if it didn't."

For his understanding, she smiled at him. "You know, you're the first person I've met here who knew Reed even a little. I'm so glad we met."

Steven reached out and relieved her of the bag of groceries. "I'll hold this for you while you find your keys."

Her lips twisted wryly. "I like your confidence."

"You'll find them. And even if you don't,

it's not the end of the world. We can get the building manager to let you in."

"Right, I know. Don't mind me. These past six weeks have been tough, and I'm afraid I've ended up with an extremely low tolerance for problems." Her fingers closed around the keys. "A*ha*, I *found* them!" She unlocked the door and pushed it open, then turned to relieve him of the sack. "Thanks for your help."

"I didn't do anything."

"I know, but it was nice to have the moral support."

"Anytime."

"Well, actually . . ." She glanced into the apartment and saw the dust motes dancing in the sunlight. Reed's apartment was located on the nineteenth floor of a Pacific Heights building that had been built in the 1930s, and its tall wide windows offered a picture-perfect view of the San Francisco Bay. A million-dollar view, Reed had bragged, the one brief time he'd brought her here.

Before leaving for the store, she had opened the windows, and now the sun and fresh air were streaming in, touching on the gleaming golden oak floors and on the boxes that were piled here and there in haphazard fashion—Reed's attempt at packing. One look at the state of the apartment last night when she had arrived had left her feeling overwhelmed, and the same feeling came rushing back to her now. It wouldn't hurt to put the task off for a bit longer.

She turned back to Steven. He was patiently waiting for her to finish her sentence. "Would you like to come in for a little while? I could make us a cup of coffee."

His stance remained casual, as if he was used to women he had just met inviting him into their apartments. "I wouldn't want to intrude."

"Are you kidding? I would take it as a favor." She smiled wistfully. "The apartment has that empty feeling of a place that's been closed up for weeks. It's kind of lonely. Having company will be good for me."

He seemed to relax, muscle by muscle. Up until that point she hadn't realized how tense he was. Strange, she thought. She kept getting mixed signals about him. For instance, there was a stillness about him, yet she would swear that he was a man of action. But whatever he was, it didn't matter. She felt comfortable with him and was grateful she had met him.

"In that case I'd love to have a cup of coffee," he said. "Thanks. Just let me put my mail in my place and then I'll be over."

"Great. I'll leave the door open."

Steven watched her whirl away into the

apartment, all energy and nerves, light and beauty. She was the color of honey all over, from her cascading hair to her gleaming complexion to her long shapely limbs. Her eyes were slightly darker, the color of sherry with a touch of pure gold. And the gold became more pronounced when she smiled or was amused about something, which seemed to happen often.

He couldn't imagine Reed having someone—even a stepsister—like her in his life. She had obviously loved him very much, yet Reed had been a complex man who never showed emotion.

In contrast, his impression of Kendall was that she was very straightforward and, unless he missed his guess, completely honest. She wore her emotions on her sleeve and he found himself wishing she didn't. There was no doubt about it, she was vulnerable. That should have made him happy, but as he thought about it his mouth tightened into a grim line.

A few minutes later the air was filled with the aroma of coffee and Kendall was handing Steven a steaming mug.

"So is there a *Mrs.* Steven Gant?" She took the chair across from him at a small table in the living room placed by a wide window.

His lips twitched at the question. The lady didn't believe in beating around the bush. Her forthrightness contrasted directly with the delicate and soft and incredibly sexy way she looked in a bright red cotton sundress that left her arms and neck bare. "No."

She eyed him with obvious speculation. "Not even an ex–Mrs. Gant?"

"No."

"How about a significant other?"

"No."

"Of either gender?"

He smiled. "No. And just for the record I'm extremely and exclusively heterosexual."

"That's good. That's very good." Mischievous laughter lit her eyes. "Wow! Imagine the women of San Francisco letting you run free all these years! There must be something seriously wrong with the water supply that's impaired their good sense."

He couldn't help it. He had to laugh. "Are you always this direct?"

"Yes. Does it make you uncomfortable?"

"No. Just disarmed."

She grinned. "That's good. I like a man who is without weapons." Of course the man sitting across from her would always be armed against a woman. His weapon was a masculinity so potent and overpowering it would capture a woman and render her defenseless before she was even aware of what had happened to her.

"Somehow I don't think there are any weapons powerful enough to ward off your charm."

Her laughter rang out, its musicality dancing in the air between them, and he felt as if he had been punched in the chest. She left him breathless.

She tilted her head to one side and her eyes twinkled. "Are you by any chance coming on to me?"

He lifted the mug to his lips and sipped, needing time to regain his composure. "Just stating the truth."

"Okay, let me get this straight. You think what you said about my charm is the truth, but you're *not* coming on to me?"

"We just met, Kendall."

"So? You could be a fast worker."

"But I'm not."

"That's too bad."

He stared at her a moment. The golden lights in her eyes were mesmerizing. If a man allowed it, they could hold him spellbound. He tried to clear his mind. "Getting back to the women of San Francisco—maybe it's their combined good sense and good taste that's kept them safe from me all this time."

Without even pausing to consider the

idea, she gave a definite shake of her head. "No, that's not it. You're obviously just very good at evading."

He'd never thought about it before, but he supposed she was right. He had become an expert at evading—and not just women. "My career has taken up a lot of my time."

"Your career? What do you do?"

He was prepared for her question. "I'm a lawyer."

"How interesting."

It wasn't just a line, he thought, bemused. She really meant it. But his profession was a subject he'd rather not get too deeply into if he could help it. "Interesting? Yeah, right. You're not going to reel off a series of lawyer jokes, are you?"

"I wish I could, but you'll be glad to know that you're safe with me. I can never remember jokes." Disgust filled her tone.

He chuckled. "You sound as if your inability to remember a joke is a real character flaw."

"Well, it is. I mean, you'd think I'd remember at least *one* lawyer joke. There are certainly enough of them around."

He nodded, a smile tugging at his lips. "I've noticed that."

She made a dismissive gesture with her hand. "Well, don't fret for a moment. Like I said, you're safe with me. Completely and absolutely."

But he wasn't safe with her, he thought. Her femininity and warmth were potent. In fact she was probably the most alluring woman he had ever met. He was going to have to proceed very carefully.

She sipped at her coffee. "So what are you doing home this morning? It's Tuesday. Shouldn't you be at your office or in court or something?"

"I'm working on a brief at home."

"Oh, and I'm keeping you from it." She took a few moments to mull over the idea. "I guess I should feel guilty, but I don't. I consider it pure luck meeting you."

Luck was the last thing that had entered into their meeting. "Why's that?"

"Because I was really dreading starting to sort through Reed's things." She waved her hand to indicate the living room where the boxes were piled. "I can't seem to summon up any enthusiasm."

"Don't you think that's normal?"

She nodded. "I suppose so, but it doesn't matter. It's got to be done."

"Don't be so hard on yourself. Give yourself some more time if you need to." He heard the words come out of his mouth and silently cursed. He should have said the exact opposite.

"I gave myself six weeks. I had to stay home for that long and finish out the school year before I could come here. I'm an elementary-school art teacher."

He nodded with interest, as if hearing the information for the first time. And it occurred to him that perhaps one of the reasons for her directness was the fact that she dealt with young children day in and day out. Most children didn't know the meaning of artifice. She would be very good with children, he decided. He also decided he needed to find a way to get back to his agenda. "Going through a loved one's possessions after he dies is not an easy thing to do, but it seems to me, all things considered, that the quicker you do it the easier it will be on you."

"Yeah, I know you're right." She gnawed on her bottom lip and gazed out at the bay. "Reed meant the world to me. Our relationship wasn't easily defined to anyone but the two of us. We weren't related by blood, but we were each other's closest living relative, and that was important to us."

"His mother is dead too?" Double-checking facts never hurt.

"Yes. His father was a widower when he married my mother. After we were grown Reed and I only saw each other a couple of times a year, but I always knew he was there for me and I hope he knew that I was there for him."

"I'm sure he did." It was strange, this need he felt to reassure her.

Her brow knitted as she remembered. "He usually came back home for visits. A few times I drove up here, but he only brought me here once to see this place. Every other time he had me stay at a hotel."

He eyed her thoughtfully. "Why? There would have been plenty of room for you to stay here. This is a two-bedroom."

"He said I'd be more comfortable at a hotel." Her brow unfurrowed and the teasing light returned to her eyes. "Maybe he didn't want me to meet you. He was the epitome of a protective big brother."

"Really?"

"Yes, really. So come on—confess. Were you living here last year? Was it *you* he was protecting me from?"

He held up a hand in denial. "Not me. I'm harmless."

She chuckled. "Right. About as harmless as a hit by a lightning bolt."

There was that directness again and it was having a twofold effect on him. He had to fight the urge to warn her to be more careful, more guarded. And he had to fight the urge to give in to her charm and float without resistance along the warm river of her sensuality. In the end he allowed himself the tiny luxury of teasing her—he couldn't stop himself. "Lightning bolt, Kendall? Is that an insult?"

"Are you kidding? Most women wait their whole lives to meet a man who makes them feel electricity, and you, Steven, are most definitely the lightning-bolt type."

He realized she had given him the exact answer he'd wanted. In fact he'd blatantly fished for it. He'd wanted badly to know she was attracted to him. And once again he was way off course. "And are you one of those women who wants to meet a man who makes them feel electricity?"

"Sure."

Slowly and with amazement he shook his head. "You know, Kendall, you really should watch what you say."

"Why?" She liked the way his lips looked when he smiled. They were full and well shaped. She would bet he would be as good a kisser as the man in her dreams. She also liked the way his long finger curled around the mug. He would be gentle when he touched a woman. Gentle, but always in control and very, very knowledgeable . . . With great effort she reined in her imagination.

"Because any other man might take what you're saying the wrong way."

"And you won't?"

"I'm trying not to."

"I admire your restraint."

A muscle moved in his jaw. "Don't."

She smiled, satisfied that he wasn't completely immune to her. For some reason, that was important to her. "But I like you. And life is too short for games." Her smile faded. "If you don't believe me, just look at Reed's life. He had everything going for him, and then *bam*, one rainy night it was all over."

The pain in her voice hurt *him*. "Yeah, I know." He searched for something to say that would bring back her smile. "But no matter what you think, I am harmless. I even open windows to let flies out instead of killing them."

"The question is not what you do to flies but what you do to women."

He spread his hands out in a gesture of innocence. "Nothing. I'm basically a very boring guy."

Her smile returned, full force. She was a golden lady, he reflected, who made him feel all kinds of dark, hot emotions. She put knots in his stomach and forcefully placed guilt in his conscience for what he was going to have to do to her.

"Boring, huh?" She didn't believe it for a minute. "Well then, I'd say that maybe it's a good thing I came along."

He was having a hard time keeping up with their conversation. One minute she was serious, the next she was teasing. She had him completely off balance, a condition he wasn't used to. "I guess now it's my turn to ask—are you flirting with me?"

She didn't even take a second to consider his question. Tilting her head so that she was looking up at him through dark brown eyelashes, she said, "Outrageously. How am I doing?"

God, she was adorable. And if he didn't get a grip on his emotions, he would be lost. And so would she. "You're doing just fine, but you're also wasting your time."

She frowned. "Why? What's wrong with me?"

He almost laughed. "There's not a thing wrong with you." He paused to choose his words carefully. "But, Kendall, you've just suffered a severe loss and I think you need a friend."

"More than I need a lover, you mean?"

There was that directness of hers again. "Well, yes."

She eyed him speculatively. "No guts, huh?"

"Good God, Kendall, you just met me!"

She laughed, unsure what she was doing but nevertheless having a great time doing it. It was the first time since Reed died that she had felt lighthearted. "Uh-huh, right—so what's your point? Haven't you ever heard of love at first sight?"

"Uh-uh." He shook his head. "You can't make me believe you've fallen in love with me at first sight."

"Okay, how about lust at first sight?"

He settled back in his chair and crossed his arms over his chest. "Do you always come on to a man like this?"

"As a matter of fact I can't remember *ever* coming on to a man like I am to you." It was the truth. She was more than a little shocked at herself, but she had meant every word about life being short. And she was *tremendously* attracted to him. "Who would have thought that my first efforts would fail so abysmally?" She waited a beat, then grinned. "And who would have thought you would fluster so easily?"

His eyes narrowed on her. "Have you been putting me on, Kendall? Is that what all your flirting has been about?"

She shrugged. "What answer is going to make you feel the best?" His eyes narrowed even more, causing her to break out into a giggle. "Okay, maybe I *am* putting you on just a little."

"Only just a little?"

Her giggle turned into a laugh. "Surely you don't expect me to tell you all my secrets. I figure if I'm to have a chance with you, I need to keep the playing field as un-even as possible."

His blue eyes flickered with appreciation. "And you're good at it. You're *very* good. Tell me something—are there any sane men left in San Luis Obispo?"

"I suppose there are a few." Her smile faded. "How do you know where I live?"

He silently cursed. "Didn't you tell me?"

"No."

"Then Reed must have mentioned it in passing."

"I thought you didn't know him well."

"I said I knew him a little."

She considered him. "You know, you're very sexy. Too bad you're such a stick-in-the-mud."

"Sorry. I've been this way since birth."

"Your poor mother."

"Never mind about my mother. Are you Reed's only heir?" He gave another silent curse. She had him so bamboozled he was being about as subtle as a jackhammer. Those lips . . . what would they feel like open, beneath his? He closed his eyes and rubbed them. For both of their sakes, he had to gain control of the situation.

"Are you trying to change the subject or are you asking that question as a lawyer? Because if you are, you can forget about getting my business for the probate. It's done."

"I wasn't asking for any particular reason —just curious, that's all."

"Yes, I'm his only heir." With a sigh she shifted her gaze to where crumpled-up newspaper from one of the packing boxes had spilled onto the floor. "You know what I can't understand? Reed was never perfect by any means, but he was never a slob either. In fact he was far more organized than I could ever be. But from the disorder here it looks as if he simply threw things into the boxes."

"Maybe he was in a hurry."

"Maybe," she said slowly. "I do know he was really happy. He was making plans to move to South America." Her gaze came back to him. "Did you know that?"

"No, I didn't," he said, managing to infuse an appropriate amount of surprise into his voice.

"He was. In fact he was set to leave less than a week after he died. He'd already bought his airline ticket."

"Was he planning on moving down there for good?"

"That's what he said. In fact a few nights before he was killed he called and told me he planned to sell most of his furniture. He didn't plan to take much with him. He said he'd buy whatever he needed down there."

"But he was obviously going to ship some things," he said, indicating the boxes with a wave of his hand.

"Some things he couldn't bear to be without. Like his record collection and books and certain things his parents had left him. Also, I guess, some clothes."

"Why was he moving?"

She shrugged. "Some sort of business venture."

"He didn't tell you what?"

"No. He was the kind of businessman who always had a lot of things going at once. He talked to me about his business only in the most general of terms. But I do know he was very successful, and whatever this particular project was he was eager to get down there. He'd even tried to get me interested in moving there."

"Would you have?"

"No. My life is here, with my friends and my students."

"I bet you're great at what you do." It was the last thing in the world he had planned to say, but he was glad he had because it earned him a luminous smile.

"I love teaching," she said simply, then turned and studied the boxes. "But I tell you what—I hate the idea of having to dispose of Reed's things. I paid the rent on the apartment for a couple more months, so I can take my time. Then again, maybe you're right. Maybe it would be easier to just tear right through the work, make the decisions, and get it over with."

He reached across the table and covered her hand with his. "I'd like to help."

For all her flirting she hadn't expected him to reach over and touch her. But he had and his hand felt right on hers. "You better be careful," she said lightly. "I may take you up on that offer."

"Good. I want you to. Sorting through everything is going to be hard and you shouldn't have to do it alone."

His dark blue eyes held hard, mysterious glints, but she wasn't bothered. "Thank you," she said with complete sincerity. "I'm very grateful."

A few minutes later, in his own apartment, Steven picked up the phone and dialed. "She's here," he said when the phone was answered on the other end. He listened for a moment. "I'm convinced she doesn't know a thing, but don't worry. I already have her confidence. This is going to be a walk in the park."

TWO

"Thank you very much," Kendall said, shaking hands with Reed's bank manager the next day. "You've been a great help."

"Please let me know if there's anything else I can do."

"I will. Thank you."

As Kendall left the bank and started toward the parking lot, her expression turned pensive. Since Reed's will had already been probated, it had been an easy matter to get the money in his checking account transferred to hers. Surprisingly there had been relatively little money in his account, but she reasoned that his low balance was probably due to the fact that he was getting ready to close the account.

He hadn't had a savings account. He *had* had a safety-deposit box, and it had contained ten thousand dollars in cash. Funny place to keep that much money, she mused. Why wasn't it invested? Maybe he had been trying to get his assets liquidated.

But, again, where was the rest of his money? He had told her that he had recently made a killing in a business deal. Was it invested somewhere she didn't know? She supposed she was going to have to turn detective and try to find it. It shouldn't prove that hard a task.

The summer wind danced around her, flirting with her lightweight gauze skirt and sending her hair dancing in the sunlight. The day was beautiful, with seagulls soaring overhead and the faint scent of brine in the air. Her thoughts returned to Steven as they had so many times since she'd met him yesterday.

She had lain in bed the night before and thought of him next door and she had wondered what he was doing. Was he lying in bed thinking about her? If he was sleeping, was he dreaming about her? They were quixotic questions, she freely acknowledged to herself. After all, no matter how at ease she felt with him or how familiar he seemed, the reality was that she had just met the man.

But she liked him. She trusted him. And she was attracted to him.

With a groan she had rolled over and punched her pillow, telling herself that she was hopeless. Eventually she had drifted off to sleep and dreamed, and the man who was in her dreams was Steven. She hadn't been surprised to see him there. In fact it seemed very natural, as if he had been lurking in the depths of her mind for some time, waiting until the time was right to reveal himself to her.

It was a rather fanciful thought, she reflected now. On the other hand, in this day and age of wanton waste it would be practically criminal to squander a perfectly good neighbor. Therefore, why not recycle him in her nighttime dreams? And while she was at it, why not take him up on his offer of help? He had said he would be home today. As soon as she got back to the apartment she'd go over and ask him to join her for lunch.

Smiling at the thought, she spotted her car up ahead and began to dig through her purse for her keys.

She was blindsided, shoved from the side with a force that sent her flying to the ground. "What—"

She fell hard, knocking the air from her lungs. Gravel bit into the flesh of her hands. She fought to breathe. Dazedly she tried to struggle up. A foot stomped down on her shoulder and kept her down. "Get it," she dimly heard someone say in a hard voice.

"Dammit, I know what to do." It was another person, the voice almost a growl.

Her purse was ripped away from her. In reflex she tried to reach out and get it back, but her hand closed around air. Her heart was pounding, the sound loud in her ears, even louder than the curse above her, even louder than the echo of the men's footsteps on the pavement as they ran away.

She had just been mugged.

The fact shocked her almost as much as the physical assault. She'd been raised in a small town and had never been touched by violence except for what she read in the newspaper or saw on television. And whenever she'd come here, Reed had been with her.

But this time she'd been alone. More than that, she'd been preoccupied, her thoughts on Steven, not on her surroundings.

Slowly she pushed herself up until she was sitting, but she knew better than to try to get to her feet just yet. She was shaking too badly.

"Hey, are you all right?"

She glanced toward the worried voice and saw a young man staring down at her. She ran a shaking hand through her hair. "I think so. I—I was just mugged. Did you see anything?"

"No, but stay right where you are and I'll go get some help."

No problem, she thought. Even if she tried to stand, she didn't think her legs would support her.

It took a little over an hour for her to recover from the mugging, or at least she was making a gigantic effort to try to convince herself that she had. She wasn't entirely certain she was being successful, though, because she hadn't even considered going to Reed's apartment. Instead she had come directly to Steven's.

And at his instant look of concern when he opened the door she realized she must still be showing signs of the effects of the mugging.

"Sweet heaven, what happened to you?" He took both of her hands and drew her inside to a sofa, settling her among the soft cushions and sitting down beside her. "Were you in an accident?" he asked urgently. "Kendall, talk to me. What's happened?"

Everyone had been very nice to her as she'd sat inside the bank's waiting room and given her statement to the police, but she'd felt very much alone. And now here was Steven, sitting close to her, the heat from his body driving away the chill of her shock, his face showing genuine concern for her.

To her chagrin tears filled her eyes. Quickly she blinked them away. "I was mugged outside Reed's bank, but I'm fine. It happened about an hour ago. Two men. They knocked me down and took my purse."

"*Damn.*" He glanced at her hands. She was holding them palms up in her lap, and he saw why. The tender skin of her palms had been torn. A dark anger gripped him. "What happened?"

Her gaze followed his. "I was pushed down to the ground. I guess I tried to catch myself with my hands."

A muscle moved in his cheek as he fought for control. He reached to lightly touch her shoulder where a large purple bruise was forming, a stain on the perfection of her smooth golden skin. "And what happened here?"

"A boot."

"One of them *kicked* you?" His eyes flashed blue sparks of fury.

Mesmerized by the sight, she nodded. Then she caught herself. "Oh, no, actually, he brought his foot down on my shoulder to keep me down."

He had to fight against the bile rising in his throat. His long brown finger trailed from her bruised skin onto the white cotton of her top and down the side of her breast to a soiled area. "And what about here?"

His touch wasn't sexual, but her heart was reacting as if it were, its beat accelerating until she felt it would burst from her chest. "It's just dirt from falling on that side."

"Are your ribs hurt?"

"I don't think so."

He let loose a string of expletives that made her blink. "Didn't anyone think to take you to the hospital?"

"I—I told them I was fine. Which I am."

"Are you sure?"

"Yes. Physically I'm fine, and I'm slowly recovering from the mental shock too."

He exhaled a long breath, then slowly lifted his fingers to her cheek, where the skin was faintly abraded. "What happened here?"

"I—I don't know. I guess my face must have hit the ground too."

When he thought of what might have happened to her . . . "Did you see who did it?"

He was shaking, she realized with surprise. He was genuinely upset at what had happened to her. "Listen, I don't want you to worry about me."

"Did you see who did it?"

She shook her head slowly, deliberately limiting her movements. Stiffness had set in, as well as a general achiness. "No, and I'm sure there's nothing wrong with me that a hot soak in the tub and a couple of aspirin won't fix." Unfortunately she didn't feel up to testing her theory just yet. For now she was content to stay where she was and let Steven fuss over her.

"Are you sure you didn't see who did it?"

"That's the third time you've asked me that question."

His tone was without apology. "Sometimes, after the shock wears off, people are able to remember small details."

"I didn't see them. I wish I had, but I wasn't able to tell the police anything helpful."

"You reported it to the police?"

"Yes, and the bank helped me notify my credit-card company. Luckily I was carrying only one. Tomorrow I'll have to go get a temporary driver's license." She managed a laugh, but it came out rather pitiful. She definitely needed to work on sounding stronger. It would certainly make her *feel* a lot better. "The two guys probably thought I'd be carrying a large amount of cash since I'd just come out of the bank. If anything good came out of all this, it's that they were bitterly disappointed."

"Excuse me?" he said, suddenly very quiet. "Did you say you were coming out of *Reed's* bank?"

"Yes. I needed to close his checking account and take care of some other stuff like that."

"I see." Indeed he *did* see and it made him madder than hell. Right now the only thing keeping him from completely losing his temper was the fact that she was safe. "I'll get the first-aid kit and see what I can do—"

"Don't bother. I washed up at the bank." At least she had tried.

"I'll get the first-aid kit," he repeated. Ice-cold anger made his actions deliberate as he rose and left the room. By the time he came back into the room, he had plotted his course of action, but he wasn't about to do anything until he had seen to it that Kendall was taken care of.

He sat back down beside her with not only the first-aid kit but a bowl of warm water, a glass of iced tea, and two aspirin. He handed her the last two items. "You haven't moved."

With a smile at his tone of approval she tossed back the aspirin. "I thought about it, but then I decided moving would be a really stupid thing to do. If a really nice, not to mention great-looking, man wants to take care of me, why not let him?"

Holding her hand over the bowl of water, he carefully sponged her palm clean. "Flirting, Kendall? Does that mean you're feeling better?"

"It means I'm *trying* to feel better."

His mouth tightened. She shouldn't be having to *try*. This never should have happened to her, but the fact that it had meant that someone was now playing outside the rules of the game. And the danger could be incalculable. "You should be more careful," he said harshly.

He wasn't only upset about her mugging, he was angry, she realized with surprise. Maybe he wasn't as immune to her as he would like her to believe, but for the moment she didn't feel up to pursuing the possibility. She kept her tone light. "Are you saying that I did something to attract the muggers?"

He spared her a glance as he turned his attention to her other hand. "No, I'm saying you should be more careful. Protect yourself."

"Fine. When you're done—*ouch!*"

"What? Did I hurt you? *What?*"

"You just hit a spot that's more tender than the rest."

"I'm sorry. I'll try to be more careful."

"You're being very gentle." And he was, unnervingly so. She was no longer a little girl complying with her parents as they ministered to her cuts and bruises. She was a grown woman sitting extremely close to a grown man who had interested her since the first moment she had laid eyes on him. In fact he was so close she could see specks of dark gray and black in his eyes. Incredibly they made his eyes an even darker blue—a deep, mysterious midnight blue.

"What were you saying?"

"I don't know." His nearness was shattering her concentration. But at least it was taking her mind off the mugging.

He slanted her a glance. "You were saying when you're done . . ."

"Oh, a gun."

He turned his head to look fully at her. "A gun?"

"When you're done with my hands I'll run right out and buy a gun." His cheeks and jaw were freshly shaved and he smelled clean, sexy, and something else. She drew a deep breath and realized she'd been right about how he smelled. His scent was dark, tantalizing, and exceedingly virile.

"Don't be silly, Kendall. When I was speaking of steps to protect yourself, I didn't mean that you should get a gun."

"A Doberman pinscher perhaps?"

"No." Taking great care not to hurt her, he dried her hands, then lightly applied salve.

"You said protect yourself and I'm trying to work with that concept." His body was throwing off a heat that was wrapping around her. His long fingers were sensitive and skilled. His hard thigh was pressed against hers. "Do you have a lot of practice in bandaging hurt women?"

"Quit changing the subject."

"Subject?" She couldn't think of a single subject more interesting than he.

"We were talking about what you could do to protect yourself."

She was tired, she realized, and sighed. "I've run through a few options, none of which you liked. So what does that leave me?" She paused to admire the deft way he was wrapping her left hand with gauze. "You're very good at this."

"Thanks."

"You're welcome. Now, where was I? Well, I can't afford a bodyguard, so maybe I should take one of those self-defense courses."

"That's not a bad idea."

"No, it's not, which is why I've already taken one of those courses. Unfortunately none of what I learned in it would have helped me today. I was blindsided."

Bastards! She was lucky she was only scraped and bruised. His frustration boiled over. "Dammit, Kendall, why weren't you paying attention to what was going on around you?"

Somehow she knew he wasn't angry at her and her reply was calm. "As I recall, I was thinking about you."

If he'd been standing he would have had to sit. As it was, all he could do was stare at her. "Why didn't you just talk to those two guys, Kendall? I'm sure you could have had them on their knees in a matter of seconds."

She grinned, feeling better by the moment. "I'll try that next time."

Shaking his head in wonderment at the ease with which she could disarm him, he turned his attention to her other hand. "I think you can get by with a bandage on this."

"Fine," she said. "Whatever you say."

His lips quirked. "Quit being so obliging. You're making me nervous."

For the first time since she had been mugged, she laughed, and it was a true laugh, filled with mirth. "Are you sure you're not involved with anyone?"

"I think I'd remember something like that." He finished putting the bandage on and looked at her. "Why do you ask?"

"Because you're so easy to get to, and I figure if I can do it, anyone can."

"Believe me, you're selling yourself short."

"What I believe is that you just gave me a compliment. Thank you."

"It was a mixed compliment."

She smiled slightly. "No, it wasn't."

She was right. Marshaling his defenses, he sat back, all business now. "Okay, you're cleaned and bandaged. Now what?"

"What do you mean?"

"What else can I do for you? Do you need food? You mentioned a bath—would you like to take it now? If you do, remember to keep your bandaged hand out of the water. Do you need to do anything immediately about replacing whatever was lost in your purse? And by the way—you said you didn't have much cash with you—were you carrying anything else of value?"

"Yes. In a little while. I will. Nope. Not really."

"Excuse me?"

"I just answered your questions."

He exhaled slowly. "Give those answers to me again. I lost track."

"Food sounds great. So does a bath, but not in the next five minutes. But when I do take one, I'll remember not to get my hand wet. Next time I get out I'll replace the cosmetics that were in my purse and whatever else I need, but there's no immediate hurry. And, no, I wasn't really carrying anything of value."

"No cash?"

"About forty dollars, plus copies of the

transactions I'd just completed. But it's okay because the bank has copies of everything."

He sat forward again. "What transactions?"

"Nothing those guys can use. I transferred the balance of Reed's checking account to mine and closed his."

"Was it a lot of money?" He caught himself. "I don't mean to pry. It's just that—"

"No, it's okay. There wasn't a lot of money, which was odd."

"How so?"

She shrugged and immediately regretted the action. The muscles in her shoulders loudly protested her movement. "I'm pretty sure Reed must have more money somewhere."

His gaze intensified. "Why do you think that?"

"Because he told me about a very large sum of money he had just made. I've just got to find it."

"Could he have already transferred it to somewhere in South America?"

"No. He specifically told me he wasn't going to do that until he knew for sure it would be completely safe. And until he got down there and studied everything from the political situation to the economy, he wouldn't know."

"So then he was going to take it with him?"

"I guess."

"But you don't know how?"

"How?" She really was extremely tired.

"How he planned to take a large sum of money to South America with him without using a bank."

She didn't understand why Steven was so interested in Reed's business affairs, but it didn't seem wrong of her to discuss them with him. She wasn't being specific about the amounts involved, and besides, Reed's business affairs were hers now and there was a thought somewhere in her aching head that maybe Steven could help her decide how best to track down the rest of the estate. If it even existed. Wearily she settled back among the cushions.

He took the hint. "Okay, food. What would you like?"

"I don't know. Something light."

"I'll see what I can do."

Her eyelids drifted downward. "I'll wait here."

"You do that," he murmured. "Rest."

When he returned from the kitchen twenty minutes later, she had fallen asleep.

He set the tray he carried on a table, then studied her. She had turned to her side, drawn her legs up, and was cuddled against the cushions. The bruise on her shoulder was fully formed now, a vicious, violent purple. The abrasion on her cheek was beginning to crust over. Her gauze-wrapped hand lay in her lap. She looked very fragile and very unguarded. Maybe the worst part was that even awake she was the same way.

What kind of life did she have that she didn't feel the need to erect barriers around her to keep her safe from the traumas and hurts of life? She'd lost family members, which had obviously been hard on her. Yet somehow she'd managed to keep an innocent and fresh spirit.

Remarkable.

Stupid.

She breathed softly, easily, her lips slightly parted. Light and shadow played in her hair. The unbruised skin of her arms and throat gleamed. The curves of her buttocks and upper thighs were hidden by the full gauze skirt she wore. But he remembered the lovely shape of her legs and the tantalizing sway of her hips as she moved. She'd kicked off her sandals, and her toes, painted a delicate pink, peeked from beneath the skirt's hem. Bruised or not, asleep or awake, she was incredibly lovely.

She made him feel emotions he hadn't felt in years. She made his heart ache. She made his loins throb.

He found himself wanting to protect her from all that was around her, including, and maybe especially, himself.

Her soul was pure, and he wasn't even sure he possessed a soul anymore.

He frowned. Was that another bruise on her upper arm? He stepped over to her and leaned down to lightly touch the suspicious area. Dammit! How had he missed seeing this scrape? When she woke he'd have to make sure it was completely cleaned.

His fingers lingered on her skin. Then, without making a conscious decision, he moved his fingers past the injury to the satin smoothness of her forearm. Heat knotted low in his stomach. She was as compelling to touch as she was to look at.

Beneath the white cotton top the rounded shape of her breasts tantalized. It would take no effort at all to lift his hand to their swell. His hand shifted until it hovered close to her upper body. . . .

He jerked upright, assaulted by the question of just exactly how much of a bastard he was. And he hated the answer he came up with.

Kendall trusted him, when in fact she should run for her life. When it came to getting what he wanted, he was a first-class bastard with very few scruples. His plan was to use her and then walk out of her life for good.

He had met her barely twenty-four hours ago, but he already knew that by her very nature she was going to be easy to use.

He also knew that by her very nature she was going to be hell to leave.

Kendall stretched awake, almost instantly aware of being sore. She lifted her hand to her head and winced at the pain.

"What's wrong? Are you hurting?"

She opened her eyes and saw Steven sitting in a nearby chair, watching her closely. "I'm just sore, that's all. How long have I been asleep?"

"A couple of hours."

She slowly straightened until she was sitting upright. "I'm sorry. I didn't mean to fall asleep on you like that."

"Your body sustained a shock. Sleep was one of the best things you could do for yourself."

"Uh-huh." She looked around, trying to get her bearings, and for the first time really took in his apartment. It was traditional and very masculine, with dark heavy woods, luxurious leather, and plush corduroy. Books and fine art lined the walls. Richly colored Oriental carpets lay on the floor. A lot of thought and care had gone into the furnishings, she reflected. In fact it had probably taken him years to get the apartment exactly as he wanted.

Everything looked perfect, but . . . "Your apartment is very nice," she said, and wondered why she felt so tentative. "You must do very well with your law practice."

"I can't complain."

"Obviously not, but I bet some of your clients complain about your fees."

He smiled faintly. "You may not remember any lawyer jokes, but you certainly know how to convey disapproval of my profession."

"I'm sorry," she said. "That was rude of me." She smoothed a hand over her hair, trying to assess the damage done by both the mugging and her nap. "I'm not used to sleeping in the daytime. I think I'm still a little disoriented."

"That's understandable. Maybe food will help. I've got you a salad in the refrigerator. Interested?"

She considered him. Even sitting still, he dominated his surroundings. His virility was quiet, but nevertheless very powerful.

She tried to analyze why she was so comfortable with him. Maybe because she was still convinced he had been the mystery lover in her dreams for the past six weeks, and it was impossible to feel awkward with a man to whom she had surrendered so completely, even if it had been in her dreams.

Or maybe the reason was even simpler: she had liked him instantly and began to want him shortly after that.

He made her pulse race and her insides heat. Teasing and flirting with him came naturally, like an instinct she had been born with but hadn't used until now. And that same instinct was telling her he wasn't the type to go out and buy Oriental carpets.

"Did you have a decorator help you with this place?"

"Yes."

She smiled. "Was she pretty?"

"She was gorgeous."

To her surprise his blue eyes were twinkling. "She probably cheated you on discounts she told you she was getting you."

"I didn't care. She smelled like magnolias."

"I hate her."

He grinned, pleased that for once he had gotten the upper hand, even if he'd had to make the decorator up. "Yeah, but you're going to love the salad I made you, if I can ever get you to say that you're ready for it."

"Did you watch me sleep the whole time?"

He exhaled a long, patient breath. "No."

"Good. I might have disgraced myself by snoring."

"You did. I heard you all the way in the kitchen."

"No, you didn't."

"No, I didn't," he agreed with another slight smile that made her wonder what he was thinking. His voice softened. "You couldn't disgrace yourself on the longest day of your life."

"Not even when I flirt outrageously with you and fail utterly?"

"Not even then."

Feeling a momentary and uncharacteristic flash of uneasiness, she regarded him solemnly. She knew in her bones that he was attracted to her, yet he tried so hard *not* to respond to her. Not that the amount or the lack of his attraction mattered. He had every right to feel and act as he wished. "I'll stop trying to flirt with you if you like."

He had to pause and think before speaking. There was the answer his gut wanted to give her and there was the answer he *had* to give her. "That would be good."

"You really want me to stop?"

Another pause. "I'd like to be friends with you, Kendall."

"So what you're saying is that you're completely immune to me?"

"Completely. Absolutely. Totally."

"Wow. *Three* adverbs. That sounds pretty definite."

"It is."

She wasn't disappointed, she realized, because for some reason, she didn't believe him. "Then I guess my plight is hopeless. I'll have that salad now, please."

"Just like that?"

"The thing about hopeless plights," she said gently, but with eyes that sparkled with humor, "is that they're so very hopeless."

"I see what you mean." He shot out of his chair and headed toward the kitchen before he could grab her and spend the rest of the day making love to her.

Last night during his telephone conversation he had said that this was going to be a walk in the park. The truth was he couldn't ever remember anything more difficult than trying to resist Kendall.

THREE

"Dammit, Marcus, I thought everyone had agreed to leave this situation in my hands. You told me I could work this my way." It was later that night and Steven was sitting alone in his study, speaking on the phone. He listened for a moment. "Yeah, well, apparently Alden got impatient. He nearly jeopardized the whole thing, and I'm telling you it can't happen again. I don't want her on her guard." Another pause. "I can do this, but I've got to do it my way in my own time. But I promise definite results." The other man gave him his assurances. "Fine. I'll talk to you soon."

He hung up the phone, leaned back in the chair, and rubbed his face. Damn. When had it all stopped being exciting and interesting? When had the exhilarating challenges turned into plain old stress? And just when had he decided he wanted out?

Very little of this situation had been handled correctly. Reed shouldn't have died. Alden should have been kept under control. One honey-colored blonde shouldn't be that much of a problem. . . .

Kendall woke the next morning feeling much better. The soak in the tub had done the trick, she reflected, swinging her legs over the side of the bed and getting up. A glance at the clock told her she'd slept an hour past her usual wake-up time, but the fact didn't disturb her. During the school year she kept a rigid schedule. On her vacations she did as she pleased.

She dressed in a gold T-shirt and a matching skort that ended midthigh, then headed into the kitchen. Minutes later she was wandering through the apartment, coffee in hand. It was time to begin sorting through Reed's things. She couldn't and shouldn't put it off any longer.

Reed had loved the good things in life and had believed in buying only the best. Consequently his stereo system was state-of-the-art, as was his big-screen television. She might take the stereo system back home with her, she mused. She'd have to think about the television set. It would be nice to see movies on a large screen, but finding room for it in her house would be a problem.

As for Reed's furniture, it was massive but elegant, upholstered in silk moiré and damask. She couldn't think of one single piece she'd like to have. Her style was a hodgepodge of small cozy, pieces of furniture that fit together casually, with a smattering of chintz and American country thrown in.

She eyed a small table constructed with twigs that looked out of place in the apartment. There was a reason for its existence. Her mother and his father had bought it for Reed while they had been on their honeymoon. They had bought her an identical one. The table would go back home with her.

Feeling chilled, she took several sips of the coffee, but it failed to warm her. She set the cup down and rubbed her arms. How she hated being here alone in Reed's apartment, knowing that she would never again see him, having to decide how to dispose of things he must have loved.

A knock at the door interrupted her musings. Steven, she thought happily. Please, let it be Steven.

And it was. Steven, virile, sexy, good-looking, wonderful.

"Good morning," she said with a warm smile of welcome, and stepped back to let him enter. Funny, she thought, she hadn't even been aware that she wanted to see him until she'd heard the knock. And then she had practically run to the door.

"How are you feeling?" His dark blue eyes inspected her.

"Fine. I soaked in the tub like I said I would and then had a very good night's sleep."

He picked up her gauze-wrapped hand. "Looks like you kept this out of the water."

She grinned. "You told me to, and of course I live to please you." She saw something dark and hot flash in the depths of his eyes, but then it was gone as quickly as it had come. She wanted it to return so that she could find out what was behind it. She wanted to experience the feeling of his eyes turning dark and hot and staying that way. She wanted him to reach out for her. . . .

He reached out and lightly touched her cheek and the healing abrasion. "I'm so sorry this happened to you," he said, his tone soft and gruff.

Heat skidded through her, touching off pleasurable sensations up and down her spine. "It wasn't your fault."

"No, but . . ." His voice trailed off and his mouth tightened. "Never mind. How about your shoulder?"

She stretched the neck of her T-shirt to

one side, baring her shoulder to him. She couldn't have explained why she had done it. She could have simply told him her shoulder was only slightly painful, and it would have been the truth. But she supposed she had wanted to tempt him. What she ended up doing instead was tempt herself; she badly wanted to feel his touch and she'd take it any way she could get it. "See for yourself."

He didn't disappoint her. Once more he reached out his hand to her, and this time his touch was so light she felt only the heat rather than the actual caress of his fingers. And it was as if she had swallowed fire.

"It looks terrible," he said, gazing down at the purple splotch staining her shoulder, his face as hard as she'd ever seen it.

"Yes." She should take some time and re-assess her feelings for him, she told herself. In an incredibly short time he had grown to be more than a helpful neighbor to her, much more. If she were wise, she would slow down and get her reaction to him under the legal speed limit. If she were wise . . . To her disappointment he pulled her T-shirt back up over her shoulder.

"You probably shouldn't do any heavy lifting until that's healed."

"It's not broken, only bruised."

"I don't care. If there's any lifting to do, I'll do it. Understand?"

"You spoke very clearly. I hear very well."

Ruefully he eyed her smile. It was a smile a man would happily follow into hell. "You think I'm coming on too strong, don't you?"

Her smile widened. "A bit. On the other hand, it's nice to have someone be concerned about me."

Somehow he had to curb his response to her. "I'm your neighbor, at least for the time being. You don't know anyone else in town. Of course I worry about you."

"How very . . . neighborly of you." In a rare act she actually paused to consider what she was about to say, but in the end she went right ahead and said it. "But guess what?"

"What?"

"I think your concern is more than that. It's got to be."

He groaned good-naturedly. "Don't start with me, Kendall. It's too early."

"Not a morning person, huh?"

"Mornings don't bother me. *You* bother me."

"That's good, that's very good."

He was growing to care about her. As strange and odd and maybe even as stupid as the idea was, she knew it was true. From the beginning and in her own way she had gone after him. She had never done anything like that before. But it all seemed so absolutely right to her that she'd felt no need for caution. Her only uncertainty stemmed from his need to keep himself from responding to her.

"Remember when I told you I'd quit flirting with you?" she asked him.

"I remember very well."

"Well, I wasn't really serious about that."

"Then why did you tell me?"

She shrugged. "I'd just been through a trauma. I can't be held responsible. So, are you staying or going?"

"Excuse me?" Her radical turns of mood left him with whiplash.

"Did you just come over to ask how I am and now you have somewhere you have to go or something you have to do? Or can you stay awhile?"

She left him without breath. "I can stay awhile."

"Great. I'll get you a cup of coffee."

"No, don't bother. I've already had plenty this morning." The sooner he got his job done, the better off he'd be. He glanced around the large room. "Have you started going through Reed's things yet?"

"Only in my mind. I plan to give all his clothes to a homeless shelter."

"I think that's a fine idea. But be sure to go through all his pockets before you do. You never know what you might find."

She laced her fingers together, unaware

of the melancholy that was shaping her features.

"I guess you're right, but that's going to be hard. Clothes are such a personal thing. Some of them probably still carry Reed's scent."

"I'll help you."

"Really? I would appreciate that."

"No problem." A muscle in his jaw flexed. He hoped he wouldn't be anywhere around when she found out how wrong she was to be so grateful to him. "What about the furniture?"

"Most of the furniture will probably go to charity or a consignment store. I'll call a couple of places before I make a final decision."

"Good, but again, before the furniture leaves here, look behind and under all the cushions." They hadn't been able to find anything, but a second look never hurt. He also wanted the chance to do some more poking and prodding, to see if anything had been sewn into any of the cushions. "I'll help. In fact I'll do it for you."

Tears stung at her eyes, and before she could stop it, a single tear rolled down her cheek. Hastily she brushed it away. "I'm sorry. It's just that I've been dreading doing this for weeks, but now that you're here, I think I may be able to get through it. You're wonderful to volunteer."

He ran a finger down the trail the tear had taken, absorbing the remaining dampness. "I'm not anywhere near wonderful," he said, the gruffness back in his tone. "Remember that and don't forget it." He saw puzzlement darken the gold of her eyes. Unwilling to answer her inevitable questions, he hurried on. "And volunteering to help you is really no problem."

"But what about your practice? It must be a busy one."

"I'll manage."

"Are you going into the office today?"

He hesitated. He had to make everything seem real. "For a few hours this afternoon."

She nodded. "Then while you're at work I think I'll go get a new driver's license. In fact, where's your office? If I get through at the DMV in time, maybe I'll drop in on you."

He stiffened. "It's not too far from here, but I'm afraid I'm going to be busy."

"Then I'll try to restrain myself and leave you in peace."

Her tone was light and cheerful and not at all offended, and his stiffness fled. He closed his fingers around her upper arms. "Don't ever be afraid to bother me, Kendall.

Promise me that you won't be. I want to help you."

His eyes were that intense midnight-blue color and there was real urgency in his voice. "Steven, what is it?"

"Dammit, just promise me."

"All right. I promise if it will make you feel any better."

He dropped his hands. "Good. Now, why don't I start going through Reed's clothes?"

"You know what?" she asked, studying him. "You're like a light signal that arbitrarily turns red, then green, then red."

He took her analogy in stride. "Yeah, but even red doesn't seem to stop you." He pointed to the bedroom door. "Come on—you can sit and watch me in case we find anything you want to keep."

As she saw it, she had two choices. One was to take him to a psychiatrist to be examined for schizophrenia. The other was to go along with him. She chose the latter. Sooner or later, she reasoned, she was going to figure him out. "Sit and watch you?" She grinned. "That won't be a hardship at all."

He went still, his face expressionless, and when he spoke, his voice sounded rough and pained, as if he had swallowed glass. "Be careful, Kendall."

The light was once again red. "Be careful of what?"

He wiped a hand over his face and for a moment she received the impression of incredible weariness. But in the next instant it vanished.

"Nothing. Forget it."

Shifting the sack of groceries she carried to the other arm, Kendall glanced over her shoulder, but she couldn't see anything out of the ordinary. So why did she feel as if someone was watching her, following her? Nerves, she supposed, and continued walking.

For most of the morning Steven had helped her sort through Reed's clothes and personal effects. He had been enormously helpful, not only because he had taken a dreaded task off her hands, but because he had done it with such sensitivity to her feelings. He had accomplished the job quickly and efficiently, but at the same time he had gently questioned her, checking and double-checking to make sure she wasn't going to regret giving Reed's belongings to charity. He had made a hard job much easier for her.

After he had left to go to his office, she had puttered around the apartment for an hour or so, then for the first time since Reed's death she spent some time in the bedroom that had served as Reed's office, going through his files and papers. The first thing she found was a letter Reed had started writing her, dated the day he was killed. It was lying squarely in the middle of the desk, as if he'd been interrupted while writing it and had left it there, intending to come back and finish it.

But he never had the chance.

She read his last words to her over and over. They were ordinary words, nothing of any import. He'd mentioned again that he really wanted her to think about moving to South America with him. It had obviously been more important to him than she had realized.

There wasn't a clue that this would be his last letter to her, and of course there wouldn't be. No one had any way of knowing. If only she'd been able to say good-bye to him, she thought, tears springing to her eyes.

Disturbed and unsettled, she gave in to the urge to escape for a while and decided to walk to the grocery store to buy the ingredients for a surprise dinner for Steven. But ever since she'd left the apartment building, she'd had the strange sensation that she was being watched, followed.

She was spooked because of yesterday's mugging, she told herself sternly. There was no one dogging her footsteps. No one. It was only her imagination working overtime.

Throwing another look over her shoulder, she saw people hurrying about their business, either in their cars or on foot. Here and there wispy gray remnants of the morning fog still clung to the ground or drifted lazily in the air. She could clearly see that no one was paying the least bit of attention to her.

She was being silly, she reflected, then recalled that after Reed had died she had experienced the same sensation of being watched. She would be parking her car in the school lot or strolling out on the school playground and suddenly she'd have the overwhelming feeling that she was being observed. But then, as now, she never saw anyone. Jangled nerves, that was all it was.

Forcefully putting her suspicion out of her mind, she walked the last block to Reed's apartment building and entered the lobby.

As she passed the row of mailboxes along one wall, the name Reed Jackson jumped out at her and brought her to a standstill. The management still hadn't taken his name off his mailbox. Of course not. He still held a lease on the apartment. He still received mail. Death didn't change that. Even without him, the business of his life continued for a little while longer. Her eyes filled with tears.

"Damn," she whispered. Just when she thought she was getting over Reed's death, something like this happened. But then again, his death would always be a hole in her life that would never mend, like the deaths of her mother, father, and stepfather.

A wave of loneliness washed over her as she touched the nameplate. As long as she had known that Reed was somewhere in the world, she had felt connected. Now she was connected to no one.

"Are you okay?" a cultured, feminine voice asked.

Hastily she brushed away the tears and turned to find a dramatic-looking woman standing before her. She had jet-black hair and dark eyes and was wearing a beautifully tailored emerald-green suit.

Kendall summoned a smile. "Yes, I'm fine, thank you." She held out her hand. "I'm Kendall Merrick, Reed Jackson's stepsister."

"I'm Marissa Mather," she said, taking Kendall's hand. "I was so sorry to hear about Reed."

"Thank you. Then you knew him?"

Marissa smiled slightly. "We went out a time or two, but I'm not sure I could say that I really knew him." She regarded Kendall with a soft, sympathetic gaze. "I suppose you're here to go through his things and empty out the apartment."

Kendall nodded. "Yes."

"That must be hard for you. I'd offer to help, but I'm on my way out of town." She waved her hand toward two suitcases sitting by the door. "Business. I'm just waiting for my taxi."

She liked Marissa, Kendall reflected, and knew a moment's pang of regret that things hadn't worked out between her and Reed. But Reed had always avoided serious relationships with women. As a matter of fact, as far as she knew he had never formed any close relationships outside his family, and she'd always had the feeling that even with his family he kept some things private. "That's very kind of you to offer, but actually someone is helping me. Steven Gant. You probably know him. He lives next door to Reed." She caught herself. "Well, I mean he lives next door to Reed's old apartment."

Marissa's smooth brow furrowed in thought. "Steven Gant?"

"Tall, broad shoulders, brown hair, great looking."

"Oh, yes, now I know who you mean. I haven't met him yet, but I've seen him once or twice coming or going. He moved into the building some time this past month."

"This past month?" Kendall shook her

head firmly. "No, you've got him mixed up with someone else. Steven has lived here for quite some time."

"Really? That's funny. I thought I'd met all the longtime residents of our building. Are you sure?"

"Very."

"Then I must have him mixed up with someone else." A horn honked outside. "There's my taxi. I'd better go." She walked to her bags and lifted them. "How long are you going to be here?"

She shrugged. "I'm not sure. A couple more weeks at least."

"Then maybe I'll get back in time to see you again." Marissa paused. "And listen, I really am sorry about Reed."

"Thank you." With a smile she watched as Marissa climbed into the taxi and it drove off. Marissa seemed like a lady she would have enjoyed getting to know better. And she would have definitely liked the chance to talk to her about Reed. Nothing specific. Just general things—little anecdotes that would make Reed seem alive again, even if only for a little while.

She started to turn back to the lobby when she suddenly froze. *Someone was watching her.* Quickly she scanned the street. Dammit, no one there seemed the least bit interested in her. Everyone was moving with purpose, talking to a friend or in a group. A mother was pushing a baby stroller. A little boy was walking his dog.

No one was watching her.

She shook her head in disgust. She was a stranger in a strange city. It was natural for her to feel a bit isolated, a bit lonely. But it was crazy to think that someone was watching her, *really* crazy.

For a fleeting moment she thought about dropping in on Steven at his office. True he had said he was going to be busy, but surely he would be able to spare five minutes to say hello. And it would be nice to see where he worked. . . .

She brought her thoughts to a skidding halt. She was coming to depend on him too much, and that wasn't good. No matter how nice he had been to her, no matter how at tracted she was to him, she mustn't take his presence in her life for granted. After all, he had had a life before she showed up—his own friends, job, family. He'd been kind and attentive to her, but she really did need to keep a grip on the reality of their situation. She had flirted outrageously with him and he had responded by being a perfect gentleman. Very disheartening, she mused.

Okay, so she wouldn't go to his office un-invited. She wouldn't flirt quite so outra-geously. She'd play it cool, as she usually did with men, and wait for him to make the first move.

With her resolve firmly in place, she headed for the elevator. Inside she punched the button for her floor and watched idly as the doors slid to a close. As she did her thoughts took off on their own. *Steven*—she couldn't wait to see him tonight.

So much for playing it cool.

FOUR

"Would you like some wine?" Kendall asked Steven after studying Reed's small but select collection of wine. The bottles were fitted into a special set of polished mahogany shelves built to hold wine. Nearly all of them were lying on their side, but three were standing upright—cheaper kinds, she guessed. "I should have offered it to you earlier, but I simply didn't think about it. I'm not much of a drinker."

He heard the question. He just wasn't capable of giving her an immediate answer. He was too absorbed in looking at her. She was wearing a simple little dress, more like a chemise, really. Made of scraps of antique lace and ivory cambric and sewn together with delicate gold ribbons, the dress was obviously one of a kind, and as far as he was concerned, so was she. She looked very feminine and fragile in the dress. She also looked damned desirable.

He could see tantalizing glimpses of skin through the small pieces of delicately worked lace and the line of her body through the fine cambric. Her neck and shoulders were bare, as were her arms, arms he could easily encircle with one hand. His mouth was dry from looking at her, but still he couldn't tear away his gaze.

"Where in the hell did that dress come from?"

She was studying a wine label but spared him a glance. "Out of my closet. I made it from scraps of dresses that were my grandmother's. Why? Don't you like it?"

He hated it because it sorely challenged the tenuous control he was managing to keep over his emotions. Truthfully he wanted to tear every scrap of it off her body. "It's fine. I just wondered, that's all."

Wanting her had become a bigger and bigger problem for him, until fighting against that wanting had turned into a constant battle. At night, he lay awake, tossing, sweating, miserable . . . and aching for her.

During the day when he was away from her, she stayed tangled up in his thoughts— sherry-colored eyes, sweet-smelling skin, glorious honey-colored hair that cascaded over her shoulders and would, he was sure, sift through a man's fingers like silk.

That he knew she was his for the asking added to his torture. When he was with her, he practically burned for her. In fact he was sometimes surprised she didn't feel the heat of his skin. Or feel his hunger for her like the palpable thing it was.

She'd *taste* as wonderful as she smelled. And being inside her with her legs wrapped around his hips would be an unbearable kind of ecstasy, worth just about anything and everything. Dying. Cheating. Lying. *Anything.*

It would be worth it to *him*—there wasn't a doubt in his mind. But once she found out who he was, it definitely wouldn't be worth it to her. She would hate him.

Taking her would be the easiest thing he had ever done. Living with the repercussions, and himself, afterward might prove impossible.

He thought too much of her to take advantage of her and that would be exactly what he would be doing if he gave in to the desire as he desperately wanted to and stole her away to some secret location where they could be alone and safe.

"Steven?"

"What?"

She held up a wine bottle, its glass so dark a green it appeared black. "Wine?"

"No thanks." Reluctantly he shifted his gaze from her to the wine. "Looks like your brother was something of a connoisseur."

"You recognize the labels?"

He nodded. "He chose well. Obviously he had a very discriminating palate."

She smiled. "He even went through a period where he made and bottled his own wine, but he gave that up as soon as he could afford the good stuff. He always took great pleasure in choosing the wine when we went out to dinner together. I tried to be enthusiastic, but I'm afraid I always ended up disappointing him with my lack of proper appreciation."

Her smile held a wistful sadness. She was thinking that there would be no more dinners with Reed, he realized. Damn Reed anyway. If the man wasn't already dead, he might be tempted to kill him for inadvertently getting Kendall involved in this sordid mess. He didn't like the sadness on Kendall's face. And he sure didn't like the fact that she was so damned vulnerable and dealing with a pack of jackals. Hell, she didn't even know what or who they were or that she was completely surrounded by them.

Worst of all she didn't know that *he* was one of the jackals.

"That wine is very expensive," he said, forcing the words past his anger. He paused, cleared his throat, then spoke again, this time infusing his tone with a casual interest more appropriate to the part he was playing. "If you're not interested in drinking it, you might want to sell it back to Reed's wine merchant." Since he'd given a wine specialist an inventory list of the wine, he knew to the penny how much it was worth. It was a very nice sum, but unfortunately it *wasn't* worth ten million dollars.

She sighed. "I'll think about it. Maybe I'll keep one or two bottles just because it would make Reed happy to know I had them."

He frowned. She hadn't made one flirtatious remark tonight. There was something wrong. "Hey, are you okay? Did something happen today that you haven't told me?"

She looked at him in surprise. "Nothing happened. Why do you ask?"

He got up, took the wine from her hand, and returned it to its place on the shelf. "You seem sad tonight, pensive."

"I'm sorry." She absently finger-combed her hair back from her face. "Am I being bad company?"

"You couldn't be bad company if you tried." He took her hand and led her to the living-room couch. It occurred to him that he had always been the one touching her. Never once had she reached out and touched him. Thank God. With every minute he spent with her, his control grew thinner and thinner. He settled himself a seat cushion away from her, as much space as he could make himself leave between them. "Okay, there is something wrong. I can tell."

Tilting her head to one side, she regarded him with a steady gaze. "I thought I was doing pretty well. You must pay more attention to me than you let on."

If she only knew. "It's not that hard. You're usually as bright and shining as a hundred-watt bulb, Kendall. This evening you've been running at about twenty-five watts. It doesn't take perfect vision to see that."

"Rats," she said halfheartedly. "So much for you paying attention to me."

"Yeah, right," he said, chiding her gently, "I don't pay attention to you. So tell me."

"It was something small, stupid really. I passed the mailbox downstairs and saw Reed's name, and this overwhelming sense of loss hit me."

"And you were surprised?"

"Yes." Shadows deepened the golden brown of her eyes. "I thought I was over my grief."

He stroked his fingers through her hair, soothing her, soothing himself. He'd been right. Her hair was like silk. "You can't immediately stop missing someone who was important in your life."

"How do you know? Have you ever lost someone important in your life?"

Too many, he thought. Way too many. But then losses were to be expected when violence was inherent in your profession. "Yes, I have," he said simply. "It's hard for anyone to get through life without losing people who are important to him."

She nodded. "I know you're right, but—"

"Kendall, you're living in your brother's apartment, going through his things. It would be unnatural to breeze through it. Give yourself a break."

She regarded him for a moment, then her somber face broke into a smile. "You're right. Thank you. You're very nice, you know."

Her smile was sweet and uncomplicated and it made him remember what a bastard he was. He dropped his hand from her hair. "So tell me about the rest of your day. Did anything else happen to upset you?" He didn't trust Alden farther than he could throw him. He saw her hesitate, as if she were thinking of something in particular. "What? What happened?"

Her expression cleared. "Nothing. You should know that—you were with me part of the day."

"Yeah, okay, but what happened after I left this morning?"

She visibly relaxed. "You know that, too, or you would if you thought about it. After I frittered away an hour or so here, I went to the grocery store, got food for our dinner, brought it home and cooked it, then when you came home I ambushed you in the hall and dragged you in here to eat."

He grinned. "I don't recall any dragging. In fact I came quite willingly."

"That's what you think. The truth is you really didn't have a choice."

"Why's that?"

"Because I left the door open this afternoon while I cooked the spaghetti sauce so that the smell would drift out into the hall and be waiting for you."

He chuckled. "Well, it worked, but you know you didn't have to cook. I could have taken you out for dinner. It would have been my pleasure."

She threw up a hand in mock exasperation. "Oh, *now* you tell me, after I practically *slaved* all afternoon."

The sparkle was back in her eyes and tied knots of need in his gut. He touched her hair again, his fingers playing with the end of a golden curl that lay over her shoulder. "Slaved? Damn, I'm sorry I missed that."

"You should be. I don't slave for just anyone."

"No?"

"No, but in your case I didn't feel like taking any chances. I figured I needed all the ammunition I had to get one of San Francisco's most eligible bachelors to come to dinner."

She was back to teasing and flirting again, which meant she was all right. Being flirted with by Kendall was more enjoyable than anything, and he'd love to play it out to its natural conclusion—taking her to bed and keeping her there until they were both exhausted and sated. But it wasn't even a remote possibility for him, nor would it ever be. And to complicate an already complicated situation, the moment he'd heard that she was mugged, he'd known he didn't have a lot of time.

He glanced around the room. "Well, you got me, so why not put me to use? How about I give you some more help this evening?"

"Nope. Tomorrow's soon enough for me to get back to Reed's things. Besides, that's not the kind of use I'd like to put you to."

"Excuse me?"

She grinned. "You think I'm shameless, don't you?"

"Actually I think you're adorable and as sexy as hell." He clenched his teeth. Even if it had been exactly what he was thinking, he never should have said it. "I didn't—"

"You do?" she asked, tentativeness in her voice. "You think I'm adorable and sexy?"

He propped his elbow on the top of the couch and rubbed his forehead. "I'd have to be a dead man not to think that, Kendall, but—"

"But? There's a but?"

Frustrated with himself and the situation, he plowed his fingers through his hair. "Dammit, Kendall. You just lost your brother. You're here all alone and I'm the only one you know. And when it comes right down to it, you don't know me. Not really."

She frowned. "Where did this nobleness come from? And *why*, for heaven's sakes? Or —wait a minute—are you just trying to let me down easy?"

"No . . . yes." He rubbed his forehead. "No."

"A man of conviction," she said sarcastically.

It was the first time she had spoken to him in that tone and he hated it. "Let's stop it right here, Kendall." Hurt flashed in her eyes and he silently swore. God, this was hard. He'd never done a job where he'd felt so torn apart. He had her confidence. If he put his mind to it, the job shouldn't take too much longer.

There was just one thing: he *had* to get past wanting her. A light sheen of sweat broke out on his forehead. "Look, I just think—"

She surged up from the couch, clearly distressed. "Never mind. You don't have to explain. I'm sorry, Steven. I don't know what's wrong with me. I've put you in a very awkward position by coming on to you like I have. You have no way of knowing it, but believe it or not it's not like me at all to be so aggressive. In fact I think I've already told you that it's never happened before. But with you it just seemed so natural."

"Kendall—"

"No, wait. I just want to add that you've been nothing but kind to me and I sincerely apologize."

He was in an awkward position, all right, but it wasn't because of anything she had done. "It's okay," he said, his jaw clenched.

She gazed down at her hands, surprised to see them twisted together. She couldn't remember ever feeling as embarrassed as she did at that moment. "No, really. I'm truly sorry. I don't think of myself as vulnerable, but I can see why you would. And I didn't mean to embarrass you. It's simply that I really, really have enjoyed getting to know you and . . . I *like* you." She gestured vaguely. "I have no explanation for it. It's just the way it is and I was hoping you felt the same way."

"Dammit, Kendall, I said *stop* it!" He reached up, closed his long fingers around her arm, and hauled her back down to the couch, this time beside him. Her soft body automatically molded to his. "I do like you. If you must know, I can hardly keep my hands off you."

"Then why . . . ?"

"Because it's not right."

"I don't understand. Right for whom?"

"For you. For me."

She shook her head, her mind in a confused whirl, her whole body alive from the contact with his. "I'm missing something here. What is it?"

"Nothing," he said gruffly. Everything, he thought. "Forget what I said. I just want to help you, that's all." But he still held on to her, his fingers rubbing the soft skin of the underside of her arm. He couldn't bring himself to break the contact, not yet.

She could argue with him, prod him, tease him, until maybe he would tell her what was behind his strange behavior. But she had no intention of forcing herself on a man who didn't want her. Even if she did want him.

She was lying against him, her breast pressed against his hard chest, and his body felt as hot as a furnace. Or was it *her* body giving off the heat? She certainly felt hot, and her heart was pounding, seeming to match his beat for beat. Her nipples were rigid points and her breasts were aching, needing his touch, his mouth. If he made even a tentative move, she knew she would go willingly into whatever realm of pleasure he chose to take her.

She was overwhelmed, she realized. Today her emotions had run the gamut from sadness over seeing Reed's name on his mailbox to desire for Steven. As a result she was way off her stride. A good night's sleep should restore her inner sense of balance; at least she *hoped* it would. She drew in a deep breath and inhaled the dark, tantalizing virility of his scent. "All right," she finally managed to say. "If you want to keep our relationship on a friendship basis, then I have to respect your wishes."

"I do."

But he flexed the fingers of the hand that held her arm, pushing them against her breast. Hunger rose in his throat, almost choking him. She wasn't wearing a bra and the dress wasn't much of a barrier. What else didn't she have on beneath the dress?

His fingers found the end of a gold ribbon. "Is this dress held together by these ribbons?" His voice was deep, husky.

"There's more to it than that."

"Not much more, I bet." He pulled on

the ribbon, unknotting the two strands. The lace and cambric parted just as he suspected and he slipped his fingers inside to her skin.

She gasped. "What are you doing, Steven?"

He was losing his mind—*that* was what he was doing. "Hush," he said, his voice tortured and thick. "Just hush for a minute and let me touch you."

His hand closed over her breast, taking her breath away.

"I have no intention of arguing," she whispered. Even if she'd wanted to, she wouldn't have been able to. Being touched by him was the equivalent of having her universe rocked.

He kneaded her breast, telling himself that in a second he would quit. He only wanted to feel the way she filled his hand and discover for himself how firm she was, how soft. If he could only do that, then everything would be all right. The hurting deep inside him would stop. The wanting.

The stiff peak of her breast teased his palm, a powerful draw, *too* powerful. He lowered his head and drew the nipple into his mouth. He planned to suckle at her breast for only a few moments. Not long at all. Only until he found out how she tasted, which he quickly did—sweet, like ambrosia. He also wanted to discover how she would react when he lightly nibbled on the nipple with his teeth.

She moaned, aching with frustration. He was driving her mad. Her fingers dug into his shoulders and she arched her back, offering herself to him more fully. And he took, drawing her nipple into his mouth and sucking hungrily. She felt feverish, wild, and leaned backward until she lay on the couch. He followed her down, turning his attention to her other breast, while his hand found its way beneath her skirt to the silk flesh of her thighs.

Soon, he vowed, he would stop. Soon. Right after he explored the heat and dampness between her legs he would definitely stop, and then everything would be fine.

Her flesh quivered as he slipped his fingers beneath the elastic of her panties and inside her. He groaned when her body accepted his fingers, then closed around them. She was hot, pulsating, welcoming, and Lord help him, he was burning up. He felt ready to explode. The intensity of his need for her was eating him alive. He wanted to put more than his fingers in her. *He* wanted to be in her, sheathed tightly, feeling her contract around him. And then he wanted to drive into her, hard and fast, until his climax ripped him apart and gave him the relief he so desperately sought.

Her fingers were clenched in his hair, holding his mouth to her breast, but with a rough sound he tore his mouth away and took full possession of her lips. It was the first time he had kissed her, but her taste was so familiar. It was the same taste as her skin, her breast, her nipple. It was the taste of Kendall and he could easily become addicted to it.

But he wouldn't. No, of course, he wouldn't.

His tongue thrust in and out, mimicking the action of his fingers. She was writhing beneath him and softly moaning.

She wanted him—the thought pounded through his brain. He could have her, make her his and his alone, relieve the pain and heaviness in his loins, restore his sanity. He could—

"Steven, please . . ." Her voice was ragged, demanding, pleading.

"Shhh," he muttered, his mouth against hers. "I just need to touch you a little while longer."

Her hands took hold of his shoulders and she began to move her hips against his fingers. Fire was racing along her nerves, and her blood was boiling and running fast through her veins. She'd never known what desire was until tonight. His deep kisses were stopping time, while his fingers manipulated her with an expertise that was driving her nearer and nearer to the brink of complete ecstasy. She could feel the hard ridge of his manhood against her and she wanted that hardness inside her. She reached for him and had the satisfaction of hearing him groan. "Do you have protection?" she whispered. She asked the question because it was the right thing to ask. But his answer wasn't important because she wanted him more than she had ever wanted anyone or anything.

Protection. The word was like ice water poured over him. He'd honestly thought touching her would be enough, yet here he'd taken them both to the edge of madness. God, what had he been thinking of?

Kendall. He'd been thinking of *her* and nothing else.

He looked down at her. Her eyes were half-closed, her lips were slightly parted, her skin was flushed, her hair was a riot of golden curls around her head. A fresh wave of lust surged through him. Her response to him had been nothing short of primitive, but then he should have known that was the way it would be. Her honesty shone through even in her passion. What you saw with Kendall was what you got.

She held nothing back, which was why he couldn't become her lover. He couldn't take what he wanted from her and then take what the jackals wanted. He couldn't hurt her, then leave her. Any other woman, maybe. But not her, not with her trust and her innocence.

Trembling, hurting so bad he felt he might die with his next breath, he eased away from her.

Blindly she reached for him. "Steven?"

He caught her hands. "We can't do this."

She stared at him, dazed by the quickness with which things had ceased between them, yet at the same time fascinated by how far they had gone. "We *were* doing it."

"No, Kendall, we weren't. And if I'd let things go any further, we would have both regretted it."

She gave a shaky laugh. "What are you talking about? I wouldn't have asked about protection if I'd thought I would regret it. I *want* us to make love."

He had her scent and moistness on his fingers. He folded them inward and made a fist. His control was in tatters. A fierce, gripping, sexual need still rocked through him. He didn't think he even had the strength to stand. "Just trust me on this, Kendall."

Inhaling a deep, steadying breath, she pushed her hair away from her face. "Trust you? How? You're not making any sense. On the other hand, I trust what just happened between us because it made perfect sense."

"Dammit, Kendall!"

Her nerves were in danger of shredding completely. "Oh, right," she snapped. *"Dammit, Kendall.* There I go again, making passes at you right and left, generally making your life miserable. You poor thing, having to put up with it. But as I recall, *I'm* not the one who started what just happened between us."

He slanted his gaze to her. Several ribbons on her dress were undone. The skirt was hiked up around her hips. Worse, a section of her dress was parted so that one breast was completely, temptingly exposed. As he remembered its taste his mouth began to water and his loins began to throb. "For God's sake, fix your dress!"

She folded her arms beneath her breasts, inadvertently pushing the luscious mounds upward. "You did the damage," she said, staring defiantly at him. "You straighten it out."

With an agonized groan he wiped a hand over his face. "What are you doing to me?"

"I guess I'm trying to drive you as crazy as you have me. Let me know when you're completely around the bend."

"I'm there," he muttered. "Fix your dress."

"No guts, Steven? You didn't hesitate to untie the ribbons. Why can't you retie them?

Or are you afraid if you touch me again you won't be able to stop this time?"

She was taunting him and she had hit the nail squarely on the head. Not being able to stop was exactly what he was afraid of.

Slowly he turned toward her and sucked in his breath. God, she was beautiful, all golden and flushed, with her eyes shooting glints of anger and her hair in sexy disarray around her head. The one breast remained bare, and its rose-colored tip captured his gaze.

She was like some pagan beauty of old, *beyond* desirable.

"Well, Steven?"

He felt himself waver. But he'd always prided himself on his iron control over any situation. More than once his life had depended on it. And in this case the stakes were higher than he cared to think about.

The jackals. If they got their teeth into Kendall's soft flesh, they would tear her apart. He might be one of them, but at least he could offer her a modicum of protection.

Trying not to think, not to see, not to feel, he reached out and mechanically pulled the dress over her breast and tied the ribbons. "There." He rose and quickly walked to the door. "I've got to go. I'll see you in the morning."

She stared after him. "Will you?"

She sounded more perplexed than defiant. He hesitated, wishing there was something he could say that would smooth the situation over with her, but he knew there was nothing. Their nerves were too raw, their passion too close to the surface. The best thing he could do was leave and give them both time and space. "Good night, Kendall."

Kendall stood beneath the stinging spray of a cold shower until her skin was numb. Then she dried off and fell into bed, exhausted. But she couldn't sleep.

She was stunned, angry, hurt, baffled. But she was no longer embarrassed or apologetic. After what had happened, there was no doubt in her mind that Steven wanted her as much as she wanted him.

She didn't know why he was holding back, but, she reminded herself forcefully, it was certainly his right. He obviously had some problems to work through. So okay.

She had no idea what would happen tomorrow, but she did know one thing: She wouldn't put herself in a position again where she was practically begging him to take her. At least she was going to try very hard not to.

Being held in the grip of that much desire

was simply too hard on her system. On her heart.

The phone rang and her nerves jumped. *Steven!*

She practically pounced on the phone. "Hello?"

But the voice she heard wasn't Steven's. It was sharp, harsh.

"You're not going to get much more time, lady. If you don't give us what we want, and soon, you're going to hate what happens next."

She groaned with disappointment. Just her luck that it was a weirdo. "You've got the wrong number, mister. But, listen, do yourself a favor. *Get a life!*"

She slammed down the phone and punched her pillow. She only hoped Steven was as miserable right now as she was.

FIVE

Steven woke after a night spent sleeping a few minutes at a time, miserable and cross and without a clue as to what to do about Kendall. He couldn't afford to feel anything; unfortunately he felt everything. Looking back, he knew things had started going wrong the moment he'd laid eyes on Kendall. The problem had been multiplied a hundredfold when he'd heard her talking to herself. Then she'd turned toward him and he'd found himself tumbling into the depths of her sherry-colored eyes.

He climbed out of bed, took a long shower, then dressed. But before he could finish his first cup of coffee, Alden showed up on his doorstep.

"What in the hell are you doing here?" Steven demanded, throwing a glance down the hall to Kendall's door. Thankfully there was no sign of her. He stepped aside. "Get in here. Don't you realize she could see you?"

Without haste Alden strolled into the apartment. "Don't worry. She doesn't know me from Adam. Not yet, at any rate."

Closing the door behind him, Steven kept his gaze firmly fixed on Alden. He was not someone you ever let your guard down with or turned your back on.

Alden was in his late twenties, with the blond, good looks of a beachboy and the sophistication to wear an Armani suit with ease. Since he was the beloved only son of the man for whom Steven was working, he had to walk a fine line with him, trying to get along with him as best he could and many times running damage control behind him.

Because Alden was also a psychopath.

"What do you want?"

"To check on your progress."

"I'm reporting to Marcus, Alden. Why don't you ask him?"

"Oh, I do. But my father thinks you can do no wrong. Fortunately I know better. You should have found our money by now."

Steven rubbed the back of his neck. "We all agreed going into this that the matter should be handled with finesse."

"I never agreed to that."

"I know, but you did promise Marcus that you'd leave it in my hands."

"I said for a reasonable period of time, *reasonable* being the key word."

"It hasn't been that long. Besides, your father is content to wait. Why aren't you?"

"Because there's no need. She knows where the money is. The letter we found that Reed was writing her clearly stated that."

"No, it didn't," he said, struggling to be patient. "Reed only said something like, *Remember what I told you. It's important.* I've never read a more ambiguous statement."

"Sure it was ambiguous. Reed was being careful. But doesn't it stand to reason he would tell her what he'd done with that money? He knew we were hot on his trail. He was getting desperate. He'd want someone else to know, just in case, and she was the closest person to him."

Steven sighed. "I'll get the money for you, Alden. But it's got to be my way. And mugging Kendall is *not* my way."

Alden shrugged. "I thought she'd have something on her that would lead us to the money. I decided to act."

"And because of it she filed a police report." Alden had always been tough to handle, but Steven thought he detected a new aspect of the volatile mix of the other man's personality. Unless he missed his guess, something bad was building up in Alden, something that was carrying him closer and closer to losing it all. Steven kept his voice quiet and reasonable as he tried to bank his own temper. The mugging proved that Alden was following Kendall. "If anything else happens she could have all kinds of law down on us, which is the last thing we want or need."

"What's the matter?" Alden drawled with a grin. "Is the kitchen getting too hot for you? If you can't do the job, just tell me. I'll take over."

Steven's eyes narrowed. "Back off, Alden. No one is doing this job but me. And if you try to interfere again, I'll have a serious talk with your father and let him take care of you."

Alden's grin faded and his lips curled into a snarl. "You're a bastard, Steven, who talks to my father too damned much. One of these days real soon he's going to realize that I'm the only one he can trust."

"Great. Fine. But until that time comes *I'm* handling this matter."

Instead of becoming angrier, as Steven expected, Alden slowly relaxed and smiled. Steven became even more worried.

"Sure. Anything you say. By the way, you aren't getting involved with her, are you?

She's really quite something. I wouldn't mind getting to know her myself."

Alden was only trying to get under his skin, Steven reflected grimly; he couldn't let him know how good a job he was doing. But he'd kill him first before he'd let him touch Kendall. "After we find the money, Alden. The money comes first."

"Good luck." Alden touched his forehead in a two-fingered salute of good-bye. "But I'm betting that you'll fail."

Steven spent the next hour after Alden left quietly assessing the situation. Alden wasn't to be trusted for a minute. He was a prince who wanted to be king, and the fact that the organization already had a king didn't bother him at all. He envisioned himself ruling his family's kingdom of ill-gotten gain right alongside Marcus, equal to him in respect and power. It was why he was so hot to find out where Reed had stashed the ten million he had stolen from them. It had galled him to no end when Marcus had chosen Steven to find the money. In fact Alden's impatience had led to Reed's death. Now he figured if he could step in and hurry the situation along, he would earn the praise and honor he so badly wanted. This only added to Steven's feeling that Alden was building toward an explosion.

It left him with little choice but to try to hurry things along. He just hoped that he hadn't screwed up too badly with Kendall last night. And he hoped to hell he wouldn't screw up again. He had to constantly remember who he was and what he was supposed to be doing. And most of all he had to remember that craving her was not part of his job.

Kendall answered her door, wearing a skinny top and short shorts that left great, tempting expanses of skin bare—midriff, throat, arms, legs. Her golden curls were piled haphazardly on top of her head and her skin looked freshly scrubbed. "Good morning," she said, a heavy dose of wariness lacing her voice.

He swallowed against a surge of desire and summoned an affable smile. "Good morning to you. Looks like you're already working."

She nodded, but made no move to invite him in.

"May I come in?" he prompted. "I have something I'd like to say to you."

She studied him solemnly. "I know what you're going to say."

"Okay, then may I come in and you can tell me what you think I'm going to say?"

"What's the point? I'm sure I've heard it before."

"You've heard *part* of it before," he corrected gently.

She hesitated. There was something different about him this morning. True, last night had given her a more intimate knowledge of him, but it wasn't simply that. It was his eyes. There was a hard resolve to them that she hadn't seen before. She had intended to avoid him, until she felt steadier and not so needy. But curiosity got the better of her and she stepped aside. "All right, come in."

As he passed her he caught a whiff of her skin and her hair and the scents went straight to his brain, fogging, distorting, making him forget.

"So what part haven't I heard before?"

His determination returned at the irritation in her voice. He turned to find her standing with her back against the door, waiting. Right, he thought. Get straight down to business. "Could you come away from the door, please?" he asked, his lips quirking. "You're making me feel as if I'm on a clock."

"You are. Unless you say or do something that makes sense within the next"—she glanced at her wristwatch—"thirty seconds, you're out of here."

"I apologize."

"That doesn't make sense." She threw another glance at her watch. "You've got twenty seconds."

"It makes perfect sense, Kendall. Come sit down."

She shook her head. "Not until you leave."

Sweet heaven, what he wouldn't give to kiss her right now. Instead he walked over to the couch and sat. "I owe you an apology, Kendall, for last night. What I did seemed like the right thing at the time, but in retrospect it really wasn't. And everything that happened was entirely my fault."

"Ten seconds."

"Forget your damned watch—I'm not leaving. Come sit down."

She tilted her head at the steel that had entered his voice. That was something new too. "I don't think so."

He sighed. "Please, Kendall."

She left the door and perched on an arm of a chair. He couldn't stop himself from eyeing the length of her legs as she crossed them. Last night, with very little effort he could have had those same legs wrapped around his hips. He passed a hand over his face, trying to recall what he had been saying. "You've got every right to be mad at me, Kendall, but please believe that I never intended to hurt you."

"I'm not mad," she said with a studied nonchalance that told him she was. "I'm not even hurt. At least not anymore. I got over all of that somewhere around four or five this morning. I just think it's best if we stay away from each other for a while, until you decide what it is you want from me."

"I know what I want from you. I want to be your friend."

"Friends don't kiss and touch each other the way you were kissing and touching me last night."

"You're right. Which is why I'm apologizing."

She tilted her head, considering him, and a long golden curl toppled from her head onto her shoulder. Absently she stuck it back in its place. "I'll be very truthful with you, Steven. I'm not sure I want you as a friend."

He fought back a wave of alarm. "Why?"

"*Because* of last night. It was wonderful. I wanted more, and because I did, I don't think I can go back to just being friends."

Why was he surprised? he wondered. *She* was the one making sense, not him. "I'd like to try."

"Why?" she asked. "I don't know where

this friendship thing is coming from, because you know as well as I do that if I came over there right now and sat on your lap, a fire would start between us and we'd be off and running."

"That's not true."

One eyebrow arched. "Do you want me to demonstrate?"

"No." For a moment he imagined the way her soft rounded bottom would feel on his lap and what it would be like to take her hips in his hands and move her against him. He lifted a hand to his forehead and found a light sheen of sweat. Lord, he should have known this wouldn't be simple. He was going to have to keep twisting the truth until he hit on a variation she would accept. "Okay, Kendall, just listen to me. There's something going on in my life right now that I really can't talk about, but—"

"Is it another woman?"

"No."

"It's not another man, is it?" Her brow pleated. "I thought I'd already asked you that."

"You did," he said wryly, "and the answer is still the same. No."

"Then what is it for heaven's sakes?"

"I'm trying to explain."

"You're doing a lousy job of it."

"Right, well maybe if you'd be quiet for a

minute, I could get through this." And maybe if she'd put more clothes on, he'd be less distracted. Maybe, but he seriously doubted it. "The thing is, I'd like to continue seeing you and helping you out with Reed's things on a friendship basis. It may be hard to keep it strictly friendship, but that's all I can offer and I'd like to think that you could respect that."

Aggravated, she smacked her hand against her bare thigh. "How can I respect something that's so dumb, Steven?"

"Because I'm asking you to. Because I want you to. Because it's important to me. Just trust me for a little while longer. Please."

She shook her head, sending the curl toppling free once more. "You're *infuriating*! It's no wonder you've stayed a bachelor for so long. You're extremely hard on a woman's nerves."

He smiled cautiously. "Does that mean yes?"

"No."

"No?" he asked, surprised.

"It means that because of you I'm not in a very good mood right now. You're asking me to accept something without a proper explanation."

"I know and I'm sorry, but—"

She held up her hand. "You apologize one more time and you're out the door."

"I can't give you a reason, Kendall."

"And I'm just supposed to accept that?"

"I wish you would."

"Well, I can't. It would actually be easier if you made up something. You could tell me there's another woman and that you've just broken up with her, but you're not quite over her and you need time. That would be easier to accept, but accepting *nothing* is hard."

"I know." He wished to high heaven he *could* lie to her, but from the first he had lied by omission and nuances, and after he had gotten to know her, it had become beyond his capability to tell her a flat-out lie. He supposed in his own way he was trying to limit his sins against her.

She eyed him thoughtfully. "You're not even saying be patient and things will change between us, are you?"

"No." He couldn't. When the job was done he was going to have to walk away, and by then she would want him to.

She got up and slowly paced back and forth in front of him, thinking. "So what you're saying is that even though I know good and damned well that you want me as much as I want you, either I accept this friendship thing or you'll walk and I won't see you again. It's got to be your way or no way." She stopped in front of him. "Is that pretty much it?"

Straightforward Kendall. Unfortunately it wasn't a straightforward matter. He wasn't prepared to walk out of her life. He couldn't, for a lot of reasons. Somehow he had to convince her to go along with him. "Nothing is that black and white, Kendall."

"Then I got what you were saying wrong? Where? What part? There was the 'I can only be friends with you' part. And you finished up with 'strictly a friendship is all I can offer.' I don't recall a part where you said there might be *shades* of friendship, perhaps *different layers*. No, it was black and white, *stark* black and white."

He exhaled a long breath. "What do you want, Kendall? What would make you happy?"

"Oh, now you're talking *me*. I guess that's some progress. Up until now it's all been about *you*."

He'd never expected her to be this tough. How incredibly stupid of him. "So do you have an answer?"

She stopped herself from answering immediately, and instead walked over to the coffee table where she'd left a glass of iced tea. She took several sips, weighing what she was about to do. She had an answer, all right. She just wasn't certain she should give it and call his bluff. Did she really have the confidence and courage to do so?

She hated games, yet here she was about to play one for the highest of stakes. She was betting that he wasn't going to be able to ignore what she believed—with just about everything that was in her—he felt for her. She sat on the floor in front of him, tucking her legs beneath her. "I want us to allow our relationship to progress naturally, without restrictions put on it by you."

His jaw clenched. Without his restrictions, she'd be flat on her back right now with him inside her. No restrictions was no good. "You'd better explain."

"Last night something exploded between us and now you want to douse water on it. That's not natural. I want to forget the 'friendship only' tag and simply see what happens."

She was so much more than he'd ever expected. If only he was exactly what she thought he was. If only this was a normal romance as she thought it was. But it wasn't.

He couldn't allow things to progress the way she wanted, yet somehow he was going to have to placate her. "You're ready to tell me to take a flying leap if I don't agree, aren't you?"

"Yes."

"You'd really do that?"

She wouldn't want to, but she didn't understand his way, and besides it was making her crazy. She'd called his bluff and she'd have to follow through. "Yes, I'd really do that."

He could hold his own with the toughest of men, but this one, soft, honey-gold woman was proving even tougher. "Okay, but how about a small compromise?"

"How small?" Her tone was cautious.

He almost smiled. He was having to fight for even an inch. "I'll forget the 'friendship only' tag and let things progress naturally, as you said, if you'll agree that we need to take things slower."

"Slower?"

"Slower. Otherwise we'll be in bed together in the next five minutes. Is that what you want?"

It was, but she didn't want to admit it and she hated that he put it so baldly. "To my mind, saying we'll go slower is a restriction."

"Not really. It would simply allow our relationship to grow at a more *natural* pace." He saw her hesitate and wanted to laugh, to shake her, to kiss her, all at the same time. If she only knew how hard this was on him. "Kendall, for crying out loud, these are dangerous times. People can't be trusted and sexually transmitted diseases are on the increase. Going slow only makes sense."

She'd won, she thought. She'd gotten him to agree to eliminate the "friendship only" restriction. Now the interesting part began—convincing him that they were right for each other. She didn't know how she knew—she just did. As far as she could tell, matters of the heart were unexplainable. "You think I can't be trusted?"

With a groan he rubbed a thumb and forefinger against his eyelids. He'd had very little sleep the night before, then he'd had the early-morning confrontation with Alden, and now this. So far his day was pretty much a failure. "That wasn't what I meant."

"Did you mean that *you* couldn't be trusted?"

"I'd just like for us to take things slowly, Kendall. I think that's a reasonable request."

"All right."

He looked at her blankly. "All right? Just like that?" He'd expected more arguments.

She laughed at his befuddlement. "You're right. It is a reasonable request. We'll take it slowly." Slow was a relative term, she reflected wryly. Still, she was willing to try.

He spread his hands out. "Well . . . good, then."

She smiled. "So how should we celebrate our new agreement?"

"Celebrate? How about lunch at Fisherman's Wharf?"

"Sounds fun."

His eyes narrowed. "Suddenly you're being awfully agreeable. Should I be worried?"

"Very," she said with a soft smile.

He *was* worried, for many reasons, not the least of which was the effect her smile had on him. She rose and reached for his hand, drawing him to his feet, not by her strength, but by her smile. "What are we doing?" he asked warily.

"We're going to start the celebration now." Sliding her arms around his neck, she came up on her tiptoes and pressed her lips to his.

He jerked his head back at the first touch. "I thought we agreed to go slowly."

"This *is* slowly," she said. "I didn't sit on your lap and I didn't pull you into the bedroom."

Yeah, right, he thought, feeling her breasts pressed against his chest. She wouldn't have to pull at all. In fact she'd only have to crook her little finger to get him to go anywhere, if it meant he could thrust deep inside her and get the absolute and complete relief only she could offer him. That was the problem. "Okay, but—"

"Oh, hush. I'm not threatening your virtue." She pulled his head down and kissed him with a directness and sweetness that weakened his knees. Automatically he put his hands on her waist to steady himself, and to his chagrin he encountered soft warm flesh. He'd forgotten about the midriff-baring top she was wearing. He dropped his hands away. She really should wear more clothes, he thought, silently cursing his inability to remain cool toward her.

But at the same time he couldn't help parting his lips for her tongue, which she'd been using to tease him with tiny darting motions. When his lips opened, her tongue thrust between them to find his own tongue, and at the contact he groaned and his hands went back to her waist.

"See?" she whispered, her soft lips against his, moving, seducing. "There's nothing wrong with us kissing, is there?"

Nothing, he thought, if he didn't mind the feeling that several nuclear explosions were going off inside him at once. He grasped her upper arms and gently put her away from him. "No," he said, going to great lengths to keep his voice even. "That was fine." He swallowed. "Why don't you change into something more . . ."

She looked at him. "More what?"

"Uh, suitable for Fisherman's Wharf. You know, more, uh, covering."

"Oh. You want to go to the Wharf *now?*"

She was disappointed that he could so coolly talk about going out to lunch right after she'd finished kissing him. The kiss hadn't been easy for her. Her insides had heated the moment her lips had touched his, and she was reduced to a mere puddle of mush. She'd like to think that he'd been at least a *little* affected.

"Why not go now? It should be nice down by the waterfront." She wasn't buying his nonchalant act, he thought. He was going to have to turn up his acting skills a notch. But in the meantime he opted for the truth. "I'm getting a headache and I think the fresh air will do me some good."

Instantly she was contrite. "Goodness, why didn't you say so sooner? Would you like something? An aspirin or a cold compress?"

He rubbed his eyes where the pain was. "If it doesn't go away after I've gotten some fresh air, I'll take a couple of aspirin."

"Okay, then. Sit down and lean your head back and I'll hurry and change."

He dropped down onto the couch, but he didn't rest his head. The aspirin and fresh air would only temporarily stop his headache, he reflected, gazing around the room. In fact he didn't expect to feel right again until he found the money and Kendall was back home in her little house in San Luis Obispo, safe and sound.

"What'd you do with it, Reed?" he muttered. "And why the hell didn't you take better steps to protect Kendall?"

SIX

A mélange of sights and sounds surrounded Steven and Kendall as they strolled along Fisherman's Wharf after lunch. The smell of freshly caught seafood mingled with that of just-out-of-the-oven sourdough bread. Up and down the waterfront people were eating crab and fish out of bowls and nibbling on loaves of bread as they walked, while mimes, jugglers, and musicians entertained.

Street vendors were offering everything from balloons to beads to sweatshirts and baseball caps. Out on the bay a small armada of sailboats decorated the water, their white sails standing out in relief against a piercingly blue sky.

Kendall curled her hand into the crook of Steven's arm. "It's a glorious day, isn't it? Like a picture postcard. I'm so glad we came down here." Suddenly she laughed out loud at the spectacle of a dark-haired little girl with chocolate smeared ear to ear, trying to squirm away from her mother, who had a handkerchief at the ready, single-minded in her intent to clean her daughter's face. "If that child has half as much chocolate inside her as she has on the outside, she may be in for a major tummy ache." She glanced up at Steven to share the enjoyment of the scene and found him frowning. "What's wrong? Has your headache come back?"

"What?" As her concern registered he quickly cleared his expression. "I'm sorry. What did you say?"

"Has your headache come back?"

"No, it's better." The pain behind his eyes had disappeared—fresh air and good food had accomplished that. But a moment ago he'd been almost certain that he'd caught a glimpse of one of Alden's men in the crowd. He would consider it a *major* headache if they were being followed. However, he wouldn't be surprised.

"Good." She squeezed his arm. "What shall we do next?"

Like a coquette, the wind played with her hair, tossing the gleaming curls into a hairdo of sexy abandon and sending the full skirt of her sundress flaring out from her legs. The sun was gilding her skin to a burnished luster. In California, where long-limbed, sun-kissed young women were the norm rather than the exception, she stood out. "You really like the Wharf, don't you?"

"Of course I do. It's great."

"You realize, don't you, that this place is nothing more than an overpriced, kitschy tourist trap?"

"So? I'm a tourist. Besides, *you're* the one who suggested it."

He grinned. "Because somehow I knew you'd like it."

"Well, I do. I love a good party, and *this*"—the wave of her hand took in the scene around them—"is a good party." She laughed again, and the sound somehow affected his heart, warming it, hurting it.

She was so easy to like, he thought. She'd be even easier to love—*if* a man allowed himself to let down his guard. "You *are* a party, Kendall."

"Thank you, but you know what? You've never really seen me at my best."

"If you get any better I'll have to start taking blood-pressure medication."

She tilted her face up to him. "Was that a compliment?"

"I refuse to answer on the grounds that it may incriminate me."

"That's being a coward."

"That's being smart."

"Uh-huh, okay, I know what we can do. Right after I buy one of those miniature Golden Gate Bridges, we can take the boat trip out to Alcatraz."

"Tour a jail? Uh, no. I don't think so."

"Why not?"

"I'm claustrophobic."

"And it would bother you to be inside Alcatraz?"

"You have no idea how much." He hoped the wry irony in his voice was evident only to him. "And besides, you're not really going to buy one of those souvenir bridges, are you?"

"I absolutely am. I'm only trying to decide whether I want one made out of toothpicks, silver plate, glass, papier-mâché, sand, or—"

"My headache's coming back," he warned with a grin.

"No, it's not." She giggled and realized it was exactly the way she had giggled the night of her college graduation when she and a group of friends had celebrated with too much champagne. This day, too, was a champagne-filled day, bubbling with possibilities. "Okay, I'll get one of the brass ones. Brass is more durable and I'll have it forever so that every time I look at it I'll remember how much fun this afternoon was."

Most of all, she'd remember him, she thought. The way her gaze always came back

to him, verifying that he was near and having
as much fun as she was. And she'd remember
how many times she instinctively reached out
to him, to hold his hand or his arm or to
simply touch him. Being with him like this
felt good and right.

And truthfully she didn't need a souvenir
to remind her of this time with him.

She took his hand and led him to a stand
with a wide variety of Golden Gate Bridge
replicas. She chose a small brass one and
reached for her purse.

He forestalled her by pulling out a money
clip of bills. "Let me pay for it. It's not every
day I get to buy a beautiful lady a bridge."

She waited until the transaction was completed and the small brass bridge was in her
purse, before she asked, "Do you really think
I'm beautiful?"

"What?" He took her elbow and moved
her into the flow of the crowd. He had just
caught a glimpse of another of Alden's men.
So there were two of them, and he and Kendall were definitely being followed, but he
was also equally positive Alden wasn't going
to make a move—not yet, at any rate. And
certainly not with him at Kendall's side. Alden's men represented no danger to them,
but being followed just plain annoyed him.

"Never mind," she said ruefully. "It's

never the same when you have to coax a compliment out of someone."

"What?" This time he looked at her.

She laughed. "I just love it when a man hangs on my every word." He was wearing sunglasses, but the lenses weren't dark enough to shield his expression from her. He looked perplexed and somewhat worried.

"I'm sorry," he said. "What did I miss?"

"Nothing important, but you want to hear something interesting?"

"Always."

She took his hand and entwined her fingers with his. "Brace yourself—you're really going to hate this."

The mischievous light in her eyes made him grin. "Lay it on me. I've had my daily dose of fresh air. I've had lunch. I've bought a bridge. I feel strong."

"Okay, here it is. I was really dreading coming to San Francisco, for all kinds of reasons. The loss of Reed, of course, was the main reason. But I also thought I'd miss my friends terribly. But I haven't and that's because of you. Right from the beginning I've felt completely comfortable with you. In fact, when I first saw you, I felt I already knew you."

"I remember." It had given him a few bad moments.

"And then I remembered *where* I'd seen you."

Suddenly oblivious to the crowd streaming around them, he stopped midstride, forcing her to a stop too. "Where?"

"In my dreams."

He should have felt relief, but her statement brought new tension. He didn't know that much about dreams, but in this case he was afraid he knew the reason he had been in hers. "Nightmares, huh?" he asked, his tone light but his gaze intent. "You must have watched a scary movie before you went to sleep. Why don't we go—"

"It wasn't a nightmare. Far from it." She stepped closer to him so that she could pitch her voice lower, for his hearing only. "You made love to me in my dreams."

"I made . . . ?" The words caused images to spring into his mind, images of the two of them, naked and flushed, entangled together amid twisted sheets, impossible to tell where one of them left off and the other began.

It wasn't her intent to be provocative. She was acting on instinct, compulsion. He was there; she could do nothing else.

She lifted her free hand and stroked his cheek, and the faint growth of his beard tickled her fingertips. "You were my dream lover for many weeks before I came to town."

Emotion was threatening to close his throat, causing his words to come out half-strangled. "You mean it was more than once?"

"It was many times. I lost count." When she had brought up the dreams, she'd had no ulterior motive. After all, they were smack in the middle of a large noisy crowd. But the talk about the dreams was disturbing him and she couldn't help but wonder what would happen if she took it a little farther. "You were very, very good, by the way."

His fingers closed around her wrist with unintended force. "Kendall—"

She laughed. "Have I embarrassed you?"

"More like bewildered me." His words sliced the air between them. He was angry, agitated, irritated. He'd never before tried to do a job where there were so many annoying complications. *Tempting* complications. Kendall, the *ultimate* complication.

"I was bewildered, too, but then I figured it out. I think I needed comfort after Reed's death, so I conjured you up."

"You conjured me up?" Trying to figure out what she did and didn't know was bringing his headache back. He dropped her hand and rubbed his forehead.

"Right. Except I didn't know it was you at first because you had no face. Have you noticed? A lot of people don't in dreams."

"It couldn't have been me," he said as firmly as he could manage. "We hadn't even met." One of Alden's men was standing by a T-shirt stand, pretending to be interested in one imprinted with the picture of Alcatraz. How very appropriate, he thought grimly.

She was past experimenting to see if she could get him to react, Kendall reflected. Now she seriously wanted him to understand. "No, it was you. When I saw you in the hallway, I recognized you—the way you stood, the slant of your shoulders, the tilt of your head. It was you. And then I looked at your hands and somehow I knew how it felt to be touched by you." She lifted his hand and lightly stroked her fingers along his palm. "And then that night after we met, I dreamed about my dream lover again, and this time I saw your face. And then when you finally touched me for real—"

He jerked his hand away from hers. "We need to go home." There were things he needed to concentrate on, things like Alden's men and how in the hell he was going to discover what Reed did with ten million stolen dollars. But he *couldn't* concentrate, not with her planting images in his head of him making love to her. It made him want her worse until the ache for her was almost unbearable.

At this precise moment he wanted her stretched out naked on a bed, or the ground or a desk, just about anything at all, as long as he was over her, plunging into her, taking her with all his force and might, expelling the hot fierce, primal need he felt for her that had been building in his body for days.

"Home?" she asked, taken aback. "Why?"

"We could probably make some real progress with Reed's things this afternoon."

She made a frustrated sound. "First of all, going through Reed's things is not your responsibility, nor should you worry about it. And second, there is no hurry."

She was wrong on both counts, he thought bleakly. "It'll be better for you to get it over with."

"Right," she agreed. "But not today. Today I want to"—she turned in a circle to see what was around her—"I want to ride a cable car."

It wasn't a bad idea, he thought. They could put distance between them and Alden's men and he could get her started back up the hill toward the apartment. "Let's go, then."

He made a last check of the two men, noting their location. The one at the T-shirt stand seemed to be getting serious about the Alcatraz T-shirt, primarily, Steven guessed, because of the pretty girl manning the stand. He should tell Alden to choose men less susceptible to women, but people in glass houses shouldn't throw stones. And right now his glass house would shatter around him if someone threw so much as a pebble.

With his hand on Kendall's back he guided her through the crowd, hoping they could slip away unnoticed, but a quick look showed him one of the men was following behind them and the other was hurrying to catch up. He wasn't surprised, but he was still determined to get rid of them.

He saw his chance as they approached a cable car. It was close to being full, but Steven spied two seats left on the bench that ran down its side. Grabbing Kendall's hand, he jumped aboard and hauled her up.

The conductor rang the bell and the cable car began to rumble up the hill. Steven glanced back and saw the two men gazing after them, their hands on their hips, disgusted expressions on their faces. He'd wave good-bye, he thought wryly, but then he'd have to explain his actions to Kendall.

"It's too bad there were two seats left," she said. "I was hoping I would have to sit in your lap."

"You're an incorrigible flirt."

"Just with you."

He believed her. Nothing she said to him or did showed experience; that she was making it up as she went along was more than evident. In fact he had the feeling she was surprising herself as much as she was him. But her inexperience didn't stop her from being extremely effective. On the contrary. "Sitting on someone's lap is probably against the rules."

"Why?"

"Safety. You could fall off."

She shook her head. "Not if you were holding me." She picked up his hand. "You've got strong hands, *wonderful* hands."

He was going to embarrass them both if she didn't stop saying whatever came into that amazing head of hers. He leaned over to her and put his mouth up to her ear. "If we don't start talking about something else, I'm going to slide this wonderful hand of mine under that sundress of yours and bring you to climax right here and now in front of all these people."

He jolted her into speechlessness, as he had hoped. So now he knew, if all else failed, he could fight fire with fire. There was just one problem. The fire was getting too damned hot, and if things didn't change between them soon, they were both going to get burned badly. Even now his fingers tingled to do exactly as he had said. And Lord, would he love it.

In fact, now that he thought about it, he'd love to have her sitting on his lap, straddling and facing him, her panties off, but her skirt covering them. Just the thought of her moving on top of him with him inside her as the cable car rumbled along a street packed with thousands of people made his blood boil and his loins harden to the point of pain.

He shifted on the bench, trying to ease his discomfort, but he knew that driving deep into her again and again was the only way he was going to find any relief and that was out of the question.

He cleared his throat and attempted a conversational tone. "Let's see, where are we exactly? It looks like—"

"Are we near your office?"

"My office?"

"Your office. Where you work. Where you practice law." She waved her hand in front of his face. "Hello? Are you with me?"

"My office isn't far from here," he said cautiously.

"How far? If we get off, could we walk there?"

He could say no and that would be the end of that. Or he could take her to his office. It would be awkward, but not a total catastrophe, if he could find a phone and call ahead. It would satisfy her curiosity and get him off this damned cable car that seemed to feed fantasies he'd never had before and he didn't know how to handle.

"We could walk it and we'd be halfway back to the apartment."

She reached for the bell cord. "Then let's do it."

BELLFORD AND GANT. Kendall read the brass plaque on the front door of the office. "Very impressive, Steven. You didn't tell me you were a *partner* in your law firm."

He opened the door and stepped aside to allow her to enter. "Don't be too impressed. It's a family firm. The Bellford on the plaque is my brother."

"Brother?"

"Half brother."

"Still . . ." She stopped talking as she absorbed the reception area. "This is very much like your apartment." Dark woods, butter-soft leather couches and chairs, fine art on the walls, and a richly colored Oriental rug.

"My brother decorated it," he said with a slight smile.

"Really? Not the gorgeous decorator who smelled like magnolias?"

"Of course not. I kept her all to myself."

She gave him a hard look. "I really hate that decorator of yours."

"So you can dish it out, but you can't take it, huh?"

"That about sizes the situation up."

He grabbed her chin between his thumb and forefinger. "Hey," he said, his voice featherlight. "There is no decorator, never has been, never will be. Okay?" He couldn't explain the need to tell her the truth about the fictional decorator, but it had been a very real need.

She smiled. "It's better than okay. It's *stupendous.*" And before he had a chance to move away, she stood on her tiptoes and kissed him.

It was a delicate kiss, with her lips barely grazing his, but its impact rocked him. Without thinking, he wrapped his long fingers around her bare upper arms and pulled her closer to him.

"Aren't you going to introduce me, Steven?"

Feeling equal portions of gratitude and irritation, he turned to the smiling man who had come up behind him. He hadn't had a chance to telephone him to warn him that they were coming, but he knew he could depend on him. "Impeccable timing as always, Mitch."

"Of course." He shouldered past Steven and held out his hand to Kendall. "I'm Steven's brother, Mitch. How nice to meet you."

"It's a pleasure to meet you too. I'm Kendall Merrick." Pleasure radiated from her face as she took in the resemblance between the two men. Mitch was perhaps a half inch taller than Steven and had the same dark good looks. His eyes, however, were a steel gray and their piercing quality was not shielded one bit by his glasses. "Steven never even told me he had a brother."

"I'm not surprised. I've always had better luck with women than he has and he's always been jealous." His hard, intelligent face softened with a smile.

Kendall liked him immediately. "I'm not sure I believe that one of you has better luck with women than the other. It seems to me you would both have an equally devastating effect on the other sex."

Mitch tucked her hand into his arm and led her toward a closed door. "I *like* her, Steven. Why haven't you brought her around to meet me before?"

"I was trying to spare her," Steven said dryly, trailing along behind them. "However, we were in the area and she insisted."

"How fortunate for me. Now we can have a nice visit. Wendy, bring us in some coffee, please."

Kendall glanced over her shoulder to see who he was talking to. She just had time to glimpse an older woman dressed in a navy-blue silk shirtwaist dress before Mitch whisked her into a spacious office.

"As a matter of fact, we can't have much of a visit," Steven said with emphasis. "We won't be staying long."

"Nonsense," Mitch said, handing her into a chair with great flourish. "I'm sure Kendall would love to hear about the time you ran out of the house, naked as the day you were born, to play in the water sprinklers, shocking neighbors and passersby right and left. Our poor sainted mother had to bribe you with ice cream to get you back inside and then had to promise to put whipped cream on top before you'd agree to put any clothes on."

"I was three years old."

"A very precocious, quite *immoral*, three, I can tell you. And then there was the time—"

Kendall chuckled. "Who's the older brother?"

"I am," Mitch said. "I'm also smarter, wealthier, and better looking."

"And you love to give Steven a hard time."

Mitch settled himself behind a vast mahogany desk. "Nothing more than he deserves. Besides, you should hear what he's done to me over the years."

"I'd like to."

"No, you wouldn't," Steven said, perching on the edge of the desk. "He lies." Even as he said it he regretted the words. They could apply so easily to him these days.

Mitch waved away his brother's accusation. "Of course I do. It's no fun otherwise."

She laughed. No amount of joking could hide the fact that Steven and his brother had a close relationship. "What type of law do you practice and is Steven wonderful at it?"

The humor slowly died out of Mitch's face and he glanced at his brother. "Corporate. Very dull stuff. And he's terrible at it."

"I'm sure it's not that dull or you two wouldn't be doing it."

"It has its moments," Steven said.

"I also don't believe you're terrible at it." Neither of the men commented, causing Kendall to look from one to the other and wonder at the new tension that had sprung up between them. Maybe at one time there had been some dissension about their specialty. She'd ask Steven later, she mused, and changed the subject. "Whose office is this? It's immaculate."

"It's mine," Steven volunteered.

She frowned. "I've never been in an office where the in and out boxes were empty and there was nothing on the desk."

"He's a neat freak," Mitch said.

That made sense to her, because it explained why he was so eager to help her get through Reed's things.

"I've been working at home," he said. "Remember?"

"I remember. We probably wouldn't have met otherwise."

Her lips curled sweetly with the memory and the expression in her eyes softened, and he wished with everything that was in him that they were alone. He was also glad that they weren't.

"When are you going to come back to the office?" Mitch asked him, drawing his attention.

"It shouldn't be that much longer. I hope to wind up things very soon."

Mitch nodded with understanding.

But Kendall didn't understand. "Why would you want to work at home when all your books and things are here?"

"Less distraction."

"But it's so quiet here." She nodded toward the phone that hadn't rung once since they'd come in.

Mitch smiled. "Maybe Steven should say, it *was* less distraction. I'm sure things have changed since you came along."

Kendall flushed. "I do feel a bit guilty sometimes. Steven's been great about helping me."

Mitch sent his brother an unreadable

glance. "I think I'll go check on Wendy and the coffee." He stood. "Kendall, it's been a pleasure meeting you."

"Thank you, but aren't you coming back?"

He glanced at his watch, then circled the desk to her. "I'm afraid I can't. I have an appointment due here any minute."

She held out her hand and he took it. "Then good-bye for now. I hope we meet again."

"Yes, me too. See you soon, Steven?"

"I'll call you."

"Good." Mitch walked briskly from the room and shut the door behind him.

Kendall eyed Steven, wondering why he suddenly seemed so thoughtful. "I liked him very much."

"I do too."

"That's obvious. Your relationship reminds me of Reed's and mine. Except that he never gave me a hard time."

"Speaking of Reed—why don't we go back home and do a little work?" He was beginning to sound like a broken record.

She rose from the chair, went to him, and put her hands on his shoulders. "What's wrong? You seem tense. Did your brother's teasing get to you?"

He looked at her in surprise. "Good grief, no."

"Then what's wrong?"

"Nothing."

Her thumbs edged up his neck and gently rubbed. "I guess the office reminds you of the work you need to do at home. You've given me so much of your time and I appreciate it more than I can say, but I also understand you have your own work to do."

She had a way of making him feel as if every nerve he possessed was exposed and hurting. She was worried about him. She had become emotionally involved with him. And she was willing to go to bed with him. It was like having a fantastic gift offered to him. All he had to do was reach out and it would be his, but he couldn't take it. And he was in hell because of it.

She slowly slipped her hands around his neck and stepped closer to him. "Steven? Look at me."

Her soft exhortation sent heat coiling through his insides. Her nearness made him feel as if he were free-falling down a bottomless hole.

But he looked at her, and what he saw made him go still. Her eyes held trust and desire, an intoxicating, dangerous combination.

"Are you sure there's nothing wrong?"

Every damn thing he could think of was wrong, but at the moment there wasn't anything he could do about any of them. She offered him comfort, relief, and an incredible sweetness, and he'd never wanted to take anything so badly in his life. "There's nothing wrong. I'd just like to get back home."

"Okay. Just one kiss and we'll go."

"No—"

She pressed her lips to his in a kiss that dissolved every thought in his head. If he hadn't been leaning against the desk, he might have fallen. She took him by surprise constantly, and his defenses against her were growing weaker and weaker.

His arms went around her, and widening his stance, he pulled her between his legs. She yielded completely, allowing him to mold her to him as if she were clay.

The desk, he thought. He could lay her on it and take her. Once and for all he'd be rid of the fever that was Kendall. Once and for all his sanity would return.

She propelled her tongue in and out of his mouth in a dance of mating. His loins throbbed heavily. She was like a bolt of electricity in his arms, and he was desperate to experience the power.

He had just started to turn her toward the desk when the office door opened.

"Where would you like me to put your coffee, Mr. Gant?"

He muttered an oath, but nevertheless he

was gentle as he put Kendall away from him. "We've changed our minds, Wendy. We don't want the coffee. Thank you."

"Very well."

He didn't look at the older woman, but he could hear the censure in her voice. He waited until the door closed again before drawing a deep ragged breath.

"Steven—"

"No," he said abruptly. "No. This has got to stop. We can't do this anymore."

She felt like crying. Her body was clamoring for him and he was rejecting her. "Why not? You want me. You can't tell me you don't."

"No, I can't."

"Then what aren't you telling me? Do you have some dreaded disease? Is that it? Is it communicable and you're trying to protect me?"

"I'm in perfect health, but I won't be much longer if we keep going to the edge and then pulling back."

She threw up her hand. "See, that's what I don't understand—*why do we keep stopping?*"

"Because an office is no place to have sex."

"Okay, I agree with that, but you also stopped in my apartment when we were alone. So there's got to be more to it than that, and I feel really stupid because I don't know what it is."

"Just a few hours ago we agreed to take things slower. I don't think we're doing such a great job, do you?"

"We also agreed to let things take their natural course."

"That natural course turns out to be way too fast for me."

"I wish I could understand you," she said, troubled.

"Don't even try. It's not worth the effort."

She crossed her arms beneath her breast, trying to hold herself together. He was right about one thing. She couldn't take much more of this frustration. "Fine. Let's go back to the apartment."

"Good," he said, relieved. "We can get some work done."

"No. I want to be alone for the rest of the day."

Damn. It would mean losing valuable time. "Kendall, we should—"

"No, there's absolutely nothing we should do today. Maybe tomorrow, but not today." Her body needed to cool off, and her mind needed to clear.

There was something very wrong with her and Steven's relationship. She didn't doubt that he wanted her. She also didn't doubt that not making love to her was hard on him. But it was also hard on her, *damned* hard.

Maybe she'd pushed their relationship when she shouldn't have. Maybe she'd jumped to conclusions without thinking things through first. Maybe he was right. Maybe theirs was not a relationship that should be consummated.

She was confused and more than a little hurt, and she badly needed time and space. And she wished with all her heart that she could stop aching for him.

SEVEN

Steven was making love to her. She arched against him as his hands slowly caressed her body, making her quiver. His hands were wondrous and skilled as always. He knew just where to touch, ever so lightly. He knew just where to press, ever so delicately, ever so sensitively. He knew just where to stroke, how much, how long. He knew how to make her cry out in ecstasy.

She was dreaming. She had to be, otherwise Steven wouldn't be making love to her. But Lord, his lovemaking was wonderful, even in a dream.

She was close to climax, her skin so sensitive one more caress would send her over the top. She strained against him, against the feeling. She was no longer made of flesh and blood, but of hot, intense pleasure. She was enveloped by fire. She *was* fire.

He was kissing her hard, as if he would devour her. He pressed his hand over her mouth. Harder. And he murmured something to her. Love words. Harsh words. His body pressed against hers. It was heavy. Her breasts ached for his touch. The pressure against her chest hurt. She cried out.

He spoke again. "Damn you, I've run out of patience. You've got no time left. Find the money or I'll kill you."

Words she didn't understand from a voice that was vaguely familiar.

Her eyes flew open. A man was sitting beside her on the bed, leaning over her. She could just make him out—the dark outline of his body against the even darker background of night, his hair a lighter color, his pale eyes glowing strangely. She screamed, but he smothered it, pressing his hand against her mouth until she could barely breathe.

"Listen to me, bitch! Find it—do you understand? Find the money or I'll kill you. That's my promise to you."

And then he was gone. Or was he still there, somewhere in the room? He'd seemed to melt into the darkness, but he could be waiting for her to see what she would do. She hadn't heard him leave. But then she also hadn't heard him enter.

Fear kept her still. She tried to listen for any sound he might make, but her heart was beating too loud and there was a scream in her throat that at any moment was going to strangle her.

Had he even been there? Had he been part of the dream? No, he must have been there. She wouldn't have dreamed someone like him. But then again, what he'd said made no sense.

Her chest rose and fell as she labored for breath. What should she do?

Steven. Steven would save her.

She bolted from the bed and raced through the rooms to the front door. *It was locked.* She didn't understand. If it was locked, no one could have broken in.

Struggling, fumbling, she finally unlocked it, threw it open, and ran into the hall, straight to Steven's apartment.

"*Steven! Steven!*" Sobbing, she banged on the door, her hands curled into tight fists. She needed to feel his strength and his warmth. She needed him to tell her everything was all right, that the man really hadn't been in her bedroom. She needed him for so many things.

He opened the door. "Kendall? God, what's wrong?"

She threw herself against him and wrapped her arms around his neck as tightly as she could. "I was dreaming." Tears slid unchecked down her face. "You were making love to me. And then this man came. His hand—he put it over my mouth and—"

"A man?" She'd awakened him out of a deep sleep and he was having trouble understanding what had happened. Had Alden really been so stupid as to terrorize Kendall? That desperate? Remembering his feeling that something bad was building in Alden, he gently pushed against her shoulders so that he could see her face, but she continued to cling to him. "Kendall, honey, calm down and tell me what happened."

"A dream. I don't—" She didn't know, didn't care. Right now it didn't matter. She was with Steven. She felt safe again and she didn't want that feeling to ever go away.

With a muffled oath, he swung her up into his arms and kicked the door shut with his foot. Long strides ate up the distance between the front door and the couch. When he tried to settle her among the cushions, she held on even tighter.

"No! Don't let go of me. Please . . ." She couldn't seem to curb the panic in her voice. It was as if she had come close to drowning, and if she let go of him she might go under again and this time not make it back to the surface and air.

"All right, sweetheart. All right." He sat

down with her on his lap. She was trembling
so badly her teeth were practically chat-
tering. He smoothed her hair away from her
face. She was too pale, he thought. "Okay,
now tell me. Did you have a bad dream? Is
that what all this is about?"

"No. Yes." She wanted to reassure him,
to banish the worry in his voice, but she was
confused. "I was dreaming and then—I
couldn't breathe. He had his hand over my
mouth."

"A man? *What* man? Are you saying that
there was actually a man in your apartment?"

"No—there couldn't have been. The
door was locked."

With a shudder she buried her face
against his neck. Dimly it registered with her
that his upper body was bare. From the
prickling of the fine hairs that covered his
muscled thighs, she guessed he must have on
just a pair of shorts. She could open her eyes
and see for herself, but that would require
too much effort. Besides, why should she?
She was in his apartment now, in his arms.
There would be no strange man here, no
nightmares.

"Kendall, for God's sake *talk* to me. Was
it a dream? I'm trying to understand." He
was having trouble keeping his temper under
control. If Alden had dared to sneak into her
apartment while she slept and had frightened

her, he was going to pay, and pay big. He didn't care whose son he was. Marcus just might be burying his son soon.

He was stroking her back, trying to calm her, but it was having the opposite effect on her. The feel of him against her own naked body had caused her blood to simmer. Naked? What was *she* wearing?

As she tried to remember she placed her mouth on the spot where his shoulder and neck curved together and heard his quick, indrawn breath. He tasted good; he smelled musky and masculine. She was wearing a silk chemise, she finally recalled, that stopped at her upper thigh.

"Kendall, try to remember—"

She stirred against him, but made no attempt to move off him. "I do remember," she murmured, keeping her eyes closed, as if what was happening were a continuation of her dream. "You were making love to me, just like you've done a hundred times before in my dreams." Her tongue flicked out and licked at his skin.

With a groan, he once again tried to push her gently away from him, but once again it didn't work. Her arms tightened around him until he could feel her nipples, hard and tight, pressing against his chest through the thin silk of her nightgown. The feeling was incendiary. How was he supposed to keep his mind on business when his body was reacting to hers in a way that had nothing to do with business and everything to do with appetites and pleasures of the body? "Kendall, honey, open your eyes and look at me. Are you awake? Look at me. I need you to talk to me."

She fastened her mouth to the sensitive skin of his neck and sucked. Because she wanted to. Because he tasted good. Because she wanted somehow to absorb him into her.

Was she asleep? she wondered. Was this a dream? Where did the dream end and the reality begin? She supposed it didn't matter. Making love to Steven *was* her dream.

"Let's make love," she whispered needily.

A taut agony gripped him. "You don't know what you're asking."

"Yes, I do. I want you, asleep, awake, any way." Her fingers skimmed upward through his hair, then holding his head, she brought her mouth up to his, finding it by instinct. "You want me as much as I want you," she murmured.

She could have no idea how much he wanted her, he thought. Sweat had beaded on his forehead and every muscle in his body was tight and hurting. He was paying a heavy price for holding back. He might have been half-asleep before, but he was fully awake now, with absolutely no excuse for wanting her so damned much.

She made a soft sound of frustration. "Kiss me back. Open your mouth."

He did, responding automatically. He didn't even know how he'd managed to resist for as long as he had. Her tongue thrust in and out of his mouth, and all he could do was shiver helplessly in reaction. His fingers opened and closed on her arms in an agitated movement. Each breath he drew seared his lungs. Each kiss she gave him set a fire in his brain.

She wasn't wearing any panties. An intense shudder convulsed through him. He could feel the rounded, bare curves of her buttocks against his thighs. He could also feel a portion of the delicate, feminine folds that hid the tiny cleft of her pleasure. He'd touched her there once before. He still remembered how silky and moist she had felt and how responsive she'd been. *She* was the dream.

Curled in his lap, all soft and warm, she was kissing him with an unbounded, uninhibited passion, and Lord help him he was kissing her back. He couldn't stop himself. She was completely pliable and willing, his to do with as he wished. She wouldn't object to anything he wanted to do to her, because he'd make sure it would be as good for her as it would be for him.

She ran her fingers across the planes of his hard chest. "Do I have to beg?" she asked with a soft moan.

He'd never felt weaker in his life. He no longer had the strength to push her away. She was silky and feminine, and he was only a man.

He wanted her and that wanting was beyond his control now. There was nothing else he could do but take her and keep taking her until his body was completely sated. He couldn't even wait until he got her into the bedroom.

With a violent desperation barely held in check, he lowered her to the couch amid the cushions and pillows. It would take a bullet directly to his heart to stop him now.

Without opening her eyes, she reached out for him. "Steven."

She said his name so sweetly, so needingly, his senses reeled. There'd never been a woman like her and he'd die if he didn't have her in the next few seconds.

He was trembling, but he managed to shuck his shorts and position himself between her legs. "Open your eyes," he said harshly. "I want you to look at me."

With a whimper she skimmed her hands down his back to his buttocks and tried to pull him to her. Resting his elbow on a cushion, he closed his fist around a handful of her gold curls. "*Look at me!* I don't want you asleep when I take you!"

She opened her eyes and looked up at him, her eyes almost pure gold. "I'm not asleep, but this is my dream."

What tiny bit of control he had remaining shredded. He drove into her, sheathing himself as deeply as he could in her tight, moist flesh. A primal growl ripped from his chest as ecstasy hit him with the force of a runaway train. He withdrew and slammed into her again, then again. He couldn't stop. He wanted to become a part of her and he wanted her to become a part of him, to bond them together irrevocably so that no one could ever tear them apart. She was an obsession, and he'd never stop making love to her, he'd never not be inside her. He was convinced that she was made for him. When he could feel the contractions of her muscles, the excitement drove him even wilder.

She strained and bucked beneath him. The pleasure she felt was all-consuming, all-enveloping. With each thrust he made, the hot sweetness grew inside her. With each thrust he made, she wasn't sure she'd be able to take another—the ecstasy was close to being unbearable. But each time she surged back up to him. The act was an instinct of survival. She had to have him in order to live.

She pleaded and cried and clawed at him. He was giving her everything she wanted and still she wanted more. She was about to come apart. She was about to fly high above the earth. She was about to know complete ecstasy.

Wrapping her legs around his hips, she held on tight. This wasn't a dream. It was too powerful, too real. And the culmination was overwhelming, an intensity of pleasure that had her spiraling higher and higher to the ultimate fulfillment.

He awoke in the night to find her curled against him, naked in his bed. Gently he rolled her onto her back and lightly trailed his fingers down between her breasts to her stomach. She was in a deep sleep, her breath coming quietly, easily, and he couldn't help wondering if she was dreaming of him.

But dreams were insubstantial things that most of the time a person never remembered. Having her beside him in bed was a reality, and he'd remember this night for as long as he lived.

He spread his fingers out over her flat belly and reflected that a baby might already be growing inside her. He'd been too caught up in their passion to think of protection, and obviously she had been too. His fingers flexed possessively on her. Lord, he would love it if she were pregnant. No matter how she hated him—and hate him she would—if she was carrying his baby, he would turn the world upside down to keep her with him.

His hand stilled on her as he reflected in surprise at the primitive feelings she brought out in him. He'd never experienced anything similar before and certainly not with a woman. When had it happened? What had made it happen? He didn't know.

She sighed in her sleep, drawing his attention back to her. The light from a full moon streamed through the wide windows and lit the room, allowing him to see her. Her hair was a mass of disheveled curls around her lovely face, her lashes were a thicket of darkness against her skin, her lips were parted and still slightly swollen from the kisses he had given her. She took his breath away, and it suddenly occurred to him that it made no difference to him whether she was pregnant or not. He would still turn the world upside down to keep her with him, but he also knew that realistically nothing he could do or say would be enough to keep her with him.

He bent to take her nipple in his mouth

and slowly, gently began to suckle. At the same time he slipped his fingers between her legs and stroked the sensitive flesh there. He couldn't find a place on her that wasn't sweet. The more he had of her, the more he wanted.

He lifted his head so that he could watch her face. He wanted to see every nuance of her reaction to his caress and he was soon rewarded. The movement was infinitesimal, a delicate quiver of her body.

He smiled with satisfaction. Finding the tight bud hidden in the feminine folds, he began to concentrate on it, increasing the pressure of his strokes until her hips began to undulate and the rate of her breathing increased.

He wanted to make love to her slowly this time, drawing out the pleasure, making the satisfaction that much more powerful. But he was already hard.

In one smooth motion, he parted her thighs, came over her, and sank deeply into her. She might be asleep, but she was ready for him, moist and warm and sheathing him tightly. And then she wrapped her arms around his neck and lifted her hips up to him.

Go slow, he reminded himself as he began to move in and out of her. Be gentle. But she was too tempting. He pulled out of her and then thrust deeper inside her, trying to satisfy the immeasurable hunger he had for her.

"Steven," she moaned softly.

It was no use, he thought, moving faster, driving into her harder. He knew firsthand how incredible the fire was between them. He couldn't go slow.

She opened her eyes and twined her arms tighter around his neck. "Oh, Steven," she whispered, "I love you so much."

She arched wildly against him, taking him deeper into her. And even when their spasms of release began, they didn't stop the movements that were as old as time. His need for her was fierce and it went deep into his soul.

When Kendall was asleep once more, Steven reflected on how she had said *I love you so much* and he had said nothing in return. Instead he had lost himself in her once again. Soon she would say "I hate you."

She thought a man had been in her apartment and he hoped she was wrong, but now that he was able to think more clearly about it, his instincts were telling him she wasn't.

He felt like the biggest son of a bitch in the history of the world.

She stirred against him. Lightly he caressed her cheek, soothing her back to sleep. Tonight she was his, but the light of day would come soon enough, bringing with it the stark, ugly truth.

EIGHT

"Here you are," Kendall said, strolling into the kitchen. "I was wondering what happened to you."

Like a plant seeking sunlight, Steven turned from the stove to look at her. She was wearing nothing more than the silk shift he had taken off her hours before, and her skin was rosy and still slightly damp from a shower she had apparently just taken. Desire surged through his loins. Amazingly he wanted her again.

She lifted her arms to comb her fingers through her hair, and her breasts rose, their nipples making the silk pucker where they touched. "I woke up and you weren't beside me." She came to him and, standing on tiptoes, kissed his cheek.

"I decided to let you sleep," he said huskily.

The smile she gave him held a knowledge of intimacy that made his pulse begin to race. She had to be thinking of the hours they had spent in the night making love.

"Finally, you mean?"

He nodded, remembering also. In fact he couldn't get those hours out of his mind. But he also couldn't afford to remember. Last night he had given in to the urgent demands of his body and lost himself in her. He had gone against all the rules of sanity, logic, and self-preservation. He had possessed her and been possessed by her, and because of it he couldn't lie to her anymore.

And he was surprised as hell at himself. He'd never *needed* to confess to anyone. But then, with her, it was all about need.

"Would you like one of my shirts to wear?" She'd be covered then and less tempting. But who was he kidding? Wearing a burlap bag, she'd tempt him.

She threw an absent glance down at herself. "No, I'm okay."

She was referring to her comfort, but in every other way she was more than okay to him. She was spectacular. He gestured to the stove. "I've made breakfast—sausage, eggs, toast. What would you like?"

She plopped down at the breakfast table.

"I'll start with coffee, but *thank* you for cooking. You're really wonderful."

With angry, jerky gestures, he switched off the gas flame and moved the skillet to a hot pad. "No, I'm not."

She gave a light laugh. "Excuse me, but I beg to differ. You not only made love to me all night, you got up and cooked me breakfast. What more can a girl ask for?"

The truth, he thought grimly. She could ask for the truth. He poured her coffee and took it to her, then sat down across from her.

"Just because I'm not ready to eat, doesn't mean you can't," she told him.

"I'm not ready to eat either. We can warm the eggs up when we are."

"Okay." Her expression turned thoughtful as she searched his face. "Something's wrong. What is it? Are you regretting what happened last night?"

"*What?*" His tone held genuine astonishment. "How could you even think that?"

She shrugged and the strap of the chemise fell down her arm, leaving her shoulder completely bare. "I don't know. You seem bothered by something."

"I've got a lot on my mind, but there is no way I regret last night." His lips drew into a tight line and he added in an undertone, "No matter what else happens."

As her brow furrowed into lines of concentration she absently slipped the strap back to her shoulder. "What could happen?"

"*You* could regret what happened last night."

She shook her head. "I can assure you that's not going to happen." He looked away and the furrows on her brow deepened. "Does what you have on your mind have to do with me?" She laughed, but it was a forced laugh, because she was beginning to feel that something was very wrong. "You look so serious. Is this where you tell me that you really do have a wife and five children stashed somewhere?"

He returned his gaze to her, his expression bleak. "No, but this is definitely where I confess to you."

A quiet dread slipped into her bloodstream. "I'm going to hate this, aren't I?"

"Yes, and you're going to hate *me.*"

She laughed shakily. "Well, then, that makes it simple. Just don't tell me." She reached for her cup again.

"I wish it were that simple, but it's not."

"Do you really have to tell me?"

"For your sake, yes. The problem is I don't know where to start."

She drew a deep, steadying breath. This was serious, though she couldn't imagine what it could be. "Okay. What exactly are your options?"

"I could start with last night. I could start as far back as Reed's death, or even before that."

"Reed's death?" Her hand jerked and the coffee sloshed onto the back of her hand. She put the cup down and sucked the spilled liquid. "What in the world are you talking about? You said you knew him only a little."

"I knew him more than a little. I had worked with him for a couple of years."

"Doing *what*? He had a lot of business ventures going—"

"Kendall, he was heavily involved with the Wharton crime family."

"Crime?" She shook her head. "No, you're mistaken. You must have him mixed up with someone else. Remember? I told you that he had different business ventures."

She was loyal and bewildered and it was breaking his heart. And the revelations were only just beginning.

"Right. Business ventures with the Wharton family. Marcus Wharton is the family's head and his son, Alden, is the heir apparent to the throne. He's the one who arranged to have you mugged. And I'm pretty sure he was the man in your bedroom last night."

The shock drained the color from her face, leaving her as pale as ash. "The man in—" The words choked in her throat as last night's terror came rushing back to her. "Are you telling me there really *was* a man in my bedroom?" She looked into his hard face and his midnight-dark-blue eyes and saw something she'd never seen before: Utter implacability. And still she couldn't accept what he was telling her. "No, no, you're wrong. The door was locked. There was no way anyone could have gotten in."

"He had a key."

The information was coming at her fast and hard, making her feel under siege. "Why didn't you tell me this last night?"

"You were in my arms. It was hard for me to think at all, so I pushed it to the back of my mind until this morning."

Tears sprang into her eyes. "Why would he have a key to Reed's apartment?"

"We had one made after Reed's death so we could search the place, just as I searched your home in San Luis Obispo."

"We . . . you . . ." Her mind shut down and a roaring came up in her ears. Steven's mouth continued to move as he talked, but she couldn't hear him. She could barely see him. Everything seemed to be fading.

She had known his scent before she had met him because he'd been in her home without her knowing it. She concentrated on trying to breathe. *In. Out. In. Out.*

Reaching across the table, he grasped her

hand and lightly patted it. "Kendall, are you all right?" She was staring straight at him, but he had the feeling that she wasn't seeing him.

Take another breath. In. Out. In. Out.

Without letting go of her hand, he rose and circled the small table to kneel beside her. "Kendall, honey, do you need to lie down? Kendall, say something. Anything."

In. Out. In. Out. Reed had worked for a crime family. Steven had searched her home. Someone named Alden had opened Reed's apartment door with a key and said some terrible things to her. *In. Out. In. Out.*

With an oath, Steven straightened and strode to the sink to wet several paper towels. Back beside her again, he lightly pressed the towels to her face. "Take it easy, honey," he murmured gently. "I know this has all been a shock, but I need you to be strong. We have a lot to do."

In. Out. In. Out. The paper towels were coarse against her skin, but the moisture felt soothing. The roaring was fading. Her vision was clearing. And she wished with all her heart that it wasn't.

"Stop," she said, her voice a raspy whisper. Weakly she lifted her hand and waved him away. She didn't want him anywhere near her.

He stepped back and eyed her with concern. "Are you all right?"

She was having a hard time comprehending the things he had said to her, but she did know one thing: It was very possible she would never ever be all right again. Bracing her hands on the table, she slowly pushed herself upright. When Steven leaned forward, his hand out to help her, she moved out of his reach. "Excuse me," she said with stiff politeness. "I'm going to get dressed."

She needed time and she needed to cover herself up to feel less vulnerable. She also desperately needed to do something normal.

"I'll come with you."

"No," she said, and, without looking at him, headed for the door.

His hand closed around her arm, stopping her. "I have to tell you the rest, Kendall."

"Get your hand off me." Each word was spoken clearly and with great emphasis.

He let his hand fall to his side. "Your front door is closed, but not locked. You left it open when you came over here. I got up in the middle of the night and closed it, but I didn't lock it."

"How thoughtful."

He hadn't known it was possible to feel this awful about himself. Frustrated, agitated, he plowed his fingers through his hair. "Kendall, I wish I could give you more time to recover from the shock of all this, but I can't. Not with Alden on the warpath. You're in danger and we've got to find out what Reed did with the Whartons' money."

Feeling as if she had stepped into someone else's nightmare, she stared at him. "Money? That's what he said on the phone, but I thought it was a wrong number. And that's what he said last night when he woke me up." She paused, trying to gather her wits. "I thought I recognized his voice."

Agony wreaked havoc with his insides, but there was nothing he could do to help himself. He had to concentrate on getting Kendall out of San Francisco safely. "You didn't tell me about any phone call."

"Silly me." Her voice was flat. "I thought it was some weirdo who had dialed a wrong number."

"Kendall, let me come with you. After you get dressed, we can talk some more."

He was the same man to whom she had given her heart and her body, she thought dully. He was the same man who time after time last night had made her go wild with ecstasy. But looking at him now, she saw a stranger. "I guess we do need to talk."

❖━━━━━❖

After she'd dressed in jeans and a long-sleeved T-shirt, Kendall sank into one of Reed's easy chairs, placing herself directly across from Steven, who was sitting on the couch. If she could have managed it and still been able to hear him, she would have stayed in the bedroom. Her body was covered, but she felt no less exposed.

She gripped the armrests. "Okay," she said slowly. "Start again."

"First let me say how much I regret having to pull you into this. I never meant to—"

"Just tell me," she said sharply.

He exhaled heavily. "I met Reed a couple of years ago when I went to work for the Wharton family."

She had to stay calm, she reminded herself. Losing her cool would do her no good. "And you said that this Wharton family is involved in crime?"

"All kinds. They operate up and down the West Coast and east to Las Vegas."

"And you think Reed was involved in something that was illegal?"

"I *know* he was, because I was right there beside him for a lot of it."

The floor beneath her seemed to shake as in an earthquake. She glanced outside expecting to see evidence that the building was swaying, but there was none. Amazing.

"So you're saying that my brother was a

criminal and that you're a criminal too?" Her voice was weak. "This keeps getting better and better, doesn't it? I can't wait to hear more."

He leaned forward and rested his forearms on his knees. He wished there was an easier way to tell her, but there wasn't. The only thing to do was get it all out fast so she could begin to deal with it all. "Look, this is what you need to know: Over a period of time your brother managed to embezzle around ten million dollars from the family. That—"

"*Ten million dollars.* Are you crazy? Reed never had that much money in his life."

"He did right before he died. That was why he was planning to leave the country. He was going to take the money and make a new life for himself in South America. But they found out about the money and confronted him. He told them he didn't have the money anymore, that he had hidden it by turning it into something else to make it easier to take with him, and that they'd never see it again. It could have simply been a stalling maneuver on his part, but I don't think it was. I think he did what he said he did and didn't believe anyone would find it. At any rate, he ran. He got in his car and sped away. He did that, Kendall, because he knew that more than likely Alden would kill him whether he returned the money or not."

"Wait a minute." She held up her hand. Absently she noticed it was trembling. "Are you saying Alden killed my brother?"

Straightening, he rubbed the heel of his hand against one eye. "Not really."

"Not really? What does that mean?"

"It was an accident, Kendall—an unfortunate accident that shouldn't have happened. It was a rainy night. Alden was chasing Reed and they were both driving too fast. Reed's car spun out of control and hit that telephone pole. He was killed instantly. He didn't suffer."

She stared at him for a long while, trying to absorb what he had said. Finally she said, "I can't think of a reason in the world why you would lie to me by telling me this preposterous story, but you've got to be."

He shook his head, his gaze fixed steadily on her. "I wish I were, but it's all true."

"You're asking me to believe that my brother wasn't the person I thought he was, but I can't do that."

God, she was hurting and there was nothing he could do about it. That knowledge made his own pain increase. "I'm sure he was in all the ways that mattered, Kendall. He loved you."

"But if what you're saying is true, he *lied*

to me all these years about what he did for a living."

"It's true, and yes, he lied to you. But he lied to protect you and he was also there for you. You told me he was."

She had to sit very still, because she was convinced that if she didn't she would fall. The floor had continued to shift and tilt, and now the room was spinning, sometimes fast, sometimes slow. It wouldn't stop and she was having to fight against a terrible dizziness and a rising nausea.

"You lied to me too," she said, her voice barely above a whisper.

He drew in a deep breath, but nothing could fortify him for what he had to say next. "Yes, Kendall, I did. And I'm sorry, but I had to get close to you. I had to get your confidence. It was my hope that you knew something about the money and just didn't realize it. Alden believed you really knew where the money was, but once I watched you for a while, then met you, I didn't."

"You . . . *watched* me?" The nausea hit her like a wall. With her hand pressed to her mouth, she raced to the bathroom and barely made it. Heaving violently, she emptied her insides into the commode, and the heaving continued even after she had nothing left in her.

When she finished, Steven was there,

handing her a washcloth. "You'll never know how sorry I am."

She grabbed the washcloth from him. Leaning back against a wall, she held the cloth to her face, and when she finally got the strength to speak, her words were muffled. "Leave me alone, Steven."

"I can't," he said bleakly. "For a lot of reasons. Brush your teeth, and I'll try to find some brandy for you."

A few minutes later she returned to the living room to find him waiting for her with a glass in his hand.

"I finally found Reed's brandy in among all that damned wine." She looked as if he'd kicked her in the stomach, and he had. He'd never been more shaken in his life. Her shock and pain was his shock and pain, though she'd never believe it.

Silently she took the glass and drank. Its fire seared down her throat and into her stomach, warming her, bringing some color back to her cheeks, and giving her system the jolt it so badly needed. She sat and stared down at the glass in her hands. "So you watched me. Where? San Luis Obispo?"

"Yes."

"So that's why I thought I knew you. I must have seen you from a distance, but it registered only in my subconscious." And then the dreams had started; hot, erotic dreams. What a fool she'd been. "And you searched my home too?"

"Yes."

So the strange feelings she had felt after Reed's death had been justified. "It's ironic, isn't it? I was completely convinced you were a good guy and then you went and turned out to be one of the bad guys."

"I've apologized, but I will again if it will do any good."

She gave a short, humorless laugh. "Yeah, right. About the only thing that would make me feel better right now is to never have to see you again."

"That's not possible. We've got to find the money."

"You can go *straight* to hell. I'm leaving just as soon as I pack." She took another drink of the brandy and waited while it traveled through her veins and settled in her stomach. Surely she'd be all right soon. Surely she'd wake up from this bad dream any minute.

"You can't leave. Alden will follow you."

"He won't be able to. I'm going to call the police."

"You can't. Bringing the law into this would put you in even more danger."

Dark sparks of anger flashed in her eyes. Surging to her feet, she hurled the brandy in his face. "*Stop telling me I can't! I can do any-thing I damned well please!*"

He'd stand there until eternity and take anything she wanted to throw at him if it would make her feel better. Calmly he took a handkerchief out of his back pocket and wiped his face. "Would you like some more brandy?"

"To hell with you. I'll get it myself." She marched over to the wine shelves and poured herself a healthy portion.

She was coming back to life, he thought with relief. Now all he had to do was get her to work with him. "Bringing in the police would be like inviting a herd of elephants to trample through a china shop."

"So the china gets broken. Who *cares*? At least you'll be behind bars where you belong, along with your friend Alden."

"Try to understand, Kendall. I wish I could sugarcoat all this for you, but—"

"Sugarcoat it? You wrapped it in barbed wire and asked me to swallow it."

"You had to know everything."

"Right. So why couldn't you have told me the truth in the first place."

"Because I was hoping I wouldn't have to. Everything would have gone a lot smoother that way."

"Smoother? Yeah, right. And I was play-ing right along, wasn't I? I'm sure you've never had anyone be so agreeable and eager." She gave a shaky laugh. "You're really a piece of work, Steven. An ugly, contemptible piece of work."

"You can call me anything you like. I deserve it all, but my goal is to get the money and keep you safe while I'm doing it, and that's what I intend to do."

She lifted her glass in a sarcastic toast. "Here is to goals. Everyone should have them. I have mine too—to get as far away from you as possible, which is what I'm going to do as soon as I finish this brandy."

What could he say to her? he wondered frantically. How could he change her mind? "I know you're angry with me, but—"

She held up her hand. "If you say one more word I swear I'm going to do something violent."

Never in his life had he felt more helpless than at this moment. He desperately needed to get through to her somehow. She *couldn't* leave. Alden wouldn't let her. His back was against the wall. He had no choices left.

"Kendall," he said, "I'm with the FBI."

NINE

Kendall stared at him without expression, but inside she felt as if she were hanging on with her fingertips to a life raft in the midst of a terrible storm and she was getting battered and beaten with each word he spoke.

"Kendall?" Concern etched his face.

"I'm not believing this," she said, carefully lowering herself into the armchair.

His instinct was to gather her into his arms and refuse to let her go until she felt better and until she had forgiven him. But he knew at the moment she wouldn't even let him within two feet of her. "Please, *please* listen to me. I've been working undercover for the past two years in the Wharton family, and I've just put my life in your hands by telling you."

"You shouldn't have," she muttered.

"You really shouldn't have. Not in the mood I'm in."

"I never meant to hurt you. Never."

"No? Well, then guess what? You failed miserably. And another thing—you may think that by telling me you're with the FBI that I'll change my mind and believe you're on the side of the angels, but you couldn't be more wrong." She gave a short, sarcastic laugh. "I know the FBI theoretically is supposed to be working on the side of right, but I never knew duplicitous behavior toward someone who has never done anything wrong in her life went along with the job description."

"Normally it wouldn't, but I'm working on both sides and you were caught in the middle. All I could do was try to protect you."

"Someone should have protected me from *you.*"

He had no defense. None whatsoever. She'd never understand the high-wire act he had to perform day in and day out.

"And why should I believe what you're telling me now, anyway? You told me you were a lawyer and I believed that."

"I *am* a lawyer, trained in corporate law. But I'm also trained in criminal law, and the law office I took you to is my brother's. I keep an office there for cover."

"Was the man I met *really* your brother?"

"Yes. He puts up with the charade against his better judgment. His hope is that I'll get tired of it all, quit the bureau, and become his partner for real."

"And the apartment next door? Is it really yours?"

"No. The FBI convinced the man who owns it to move out temporarily and paid him handsomely for his trouble. I told the Whartons *I* had made the arrangements and moved in a month before you did." His lips quirked mirthlessly. "Marcus was very pleased with my initiative. Alden was ready to bite bullets."

"So Marissa was right. You had just moved in. I feel so dumb, but then I guess I shouldn't. You're very, very good."

"I have to be. At any given time my life could depend on it."

"How very dramatic. Tell me something, Steven. How does the government of these United States view an FBI agent sleeping with one of his victims?"

A muscle in his jaw jerked. "They'd view it very dimly and you're not my victim."

"Really? Then why do I feel like I am?"

He shook his head with regret. "For your sake I should never have made love to you last night, Kendall. But . . . I couldn't help myself." The admission came hard. He wasn't used to losing control. And he wasn't used to knowing that even though making love to her had been a mistake, he'd do it all again if he had the chance.

She wiped a hand over her eyes, wishing the gesture would banish him from her sight. "I guess I should take the blame for that, shouldn't I? As I recall, I practically begged you."

"It wasn't your fault. I knew better. And you didn't have to beg. I've never wanted a woman like I wanted you."

She looked at him. A day ago the admission would have delighted her. Now it only sickened her. He'd become her lover last night, but right from the beginning he had been deceiving her. She couldn't trust a thing he said. "What kind of man are you that can live a lie day in and day out?"

"The kind of man who has always believed in what he's doing and is very good at what he does."

"And the end justifies the means?"

"Up until now it has."

"I suppose you think of your work as noble, righting the wrongs of the world."

"There's nothing noble about it. It's down and dirty and at times horrifyingly gut twisting. No one should have to do it. But the unfortunate reality is that the need is

there. And for both of our sakes I have to ask
you to try to understand."

Her laugh was knife sharp. "You're kidding, right?" The nightmare kept getting
worse and worse. When was it going to end?

"I'm not kidding about a damned thing."
He sank onto the sofa and gazed bleakly at
her. "You need to understand that people
like the Whartons are very suspicious people.
They have to be because someone they think
of as a friend today could stick a knife in
their back tomorrow."

"Like you, you mean?" she asked sarcastically.

"Marcus doesn't completely trust me, not
really. But I've made myself very useful to
him and so he uses me. At the same time I've
used him to gather information for an indictment against him and his entire organization.
But all along I've had to be extremely careful.
I've never been able to let my emotions rule
me, because one wrong step, one wrong
word, and I'd be dead. It's been a life-or-
death masquerade."

"And that's what it's been with me, hasn't
it?" she asked dully. "A lousy masquerade."

"It was better for you not to know. It
would still be better, but I ran out of time."

"What a shame. And I'm sure you had it
all so carefully planned."

He made a sound of frustration. "I know

I've given you a lot to digest, but you've got to realize that the knowledge I just gave you is very dangerous to both of us."

She shook her head. "Not to me, because I'm going to get on a plane and go as far away from here as I can."

"Alden has been trying to impress his father his whole life and he considers this his big chance. He'd chase you to the ends of the earth for that ten million."

"I don't *have* it."

"Yes, you do. You just don't know that you do."

She was suddenly very weary. "All right, fine. Whatever you say. I'm sure you're right. After all, you're a good guy who disguises himself as a bad guy and my brother was a bad guy who disguised himself as a good guy. It all makes perfect sense. I'll tell you what." The wave of her hand encompassed the entire apartment. "You can have everything in here. The entire contents. More power to you if you can find ten million dollars."

He shook his head. "Kendall, honey, listen to me."

"Don't call me honey!"

"All right, all right." His tone was soothing, pacifying. "You're right. I shouldn't call you that. But please understand that Alden is not going to let you go anywhere."

He kept asking her to understand, she

thought, but at the moment it was like asking her to step out the tenth-floor window and fly. She jumped up and began pacing. "If any of this is remotely the truth, I am not involved, never have been, never will be."

"Reed involved you when he made you his heir."

With her mind racing a hundred different ways at once, she stopped in front of him. "You say you're with the FBI? Then I want to talk to the director right now. I pay taxes. I'm a United States citizen. This is the United States. That means I'm free to go wherever the hell I please." She knew she wasn't being reasonable, but then this wasn't a reasonable situation.

Steven let out a long breath. "What can I say to get through to you?"

"Nothing. Just get the director on the phone for me—no, better yet, the *president*. He can call out the marines and they can invade San Francisco and take the Wharton family into custody and then everything will be solved."

"It wouldn't solve a thing."

She gave him a dark look. "Why not? It makes as much sense as anything you're saying."

"The ten million dollars Reed took is still somewhere and the FBI wants it as another nail in the Wharton's coffin. When the

Whartons go down we don't want them to get up again."

"And how will finding the ten million do that?"

"We're not sure yet, because we don't know what Reed did with it."

"And so we're going through all of this over something you're not sure of."

"We're sure Reed took the money, making it money that was illegally gotten twice, once by the Whartons and once by Reed. It's just a matter of finding it and tracing it. The difficulty in pinning this on the Whartons is that Reed effectively laundered the money by converting the cash into something else. But if we can find whatever it is, we have a chance to overcome that difficulty."

She stared at him. "Reed was a good man."

"He was a good brother, but he wasn't such a good man."

Her hands tightened into fists. "*Why* should I believe you? Give me one good reason."

"Where's the phone book?"

She blinked. "The *what*?"

"The phone book."

She was so astonished by his request that she automatically pointed toward the kitchen, then watched him disappear into that room.

In less than a minute he was back, carrying the thick phone book. He put it down on the table by the window. "Would you please come here? I want you to look up the number of the Federal Bureau of Investigation."

"Why?" She felt so stupid. Would she ever understand anything again? Would she ever be able to believe in anything or anybody again?

"I want you to see the number for yourself so that there'll be no way I can trick you. And I want you to dial the number yourself. My supervisor's name is Michael McMurphy. Ask for him."

She did it, not because he had asked her to, but because she needed to know. After Steven spoke briefly to Agent McMurphy, giving him a thumbnail sketch of the situation, the man verified Steven's identity to her. He was who he said he was. And knowing it didn't make her feel one bit better.

"Well?" he asked when she had hung up the phone.

She was holding herself together with only the greatest of efforts. "Get out, Steven. Just get out."

"I can't."

She walked to the door and opened it. "Yes, you can. It's real easy. Just put one foot in front of the other and leave. I need time to think, but most of all I need time away from you."

His hesitation was unmistakable.

"I have to have time, Steven, and if you don't give it to me, I'm going home, and if Alden wants to come after me, then so be it."

"You have no idea what you'd be inviting."

"Maybe not, but at least I'd be expecting him. *You*, I wasn't expecting at all. You blindsided me, Steven, and now I need a little time to try to recover and put my thoughts into some kind of order."

"Okay," he said reluctantly. "But don't take too much time. We simply don't have it. I'll be right next door if you need me."

"You'll have to excuse me if I don't find that thought at all comforting."

Kendall walked slowly through the apartment, gazing at all the things that Reed had chosen to surround himself with, things that he had loved—his records, his stereo system, his wine collection. It was hard for her to believe everything had really been gotten with money earned illegally, but as much as she didn't want to believe Steven, she supposed she had to.

She also didn't want to see Steven ever

again, but she supposed she had to do that too. Because it was in her best interest.

She almost laughed at that thought. *Her best interest*. How could it be in her best interest to work with Steven, the man who had made passionate love to her just hours before to find what amounted to the illegal gains of her brother.

Her heart hurt every time she thought about Steven's deception. To her knowledge she'd never been betrayed before. But then apparently Reed had deceived her all along about what he had done for a living.

When she looked back, there were things she had chalked up to his being overly protective of her that she could now interpret another way. The fact that he always wanted her to stay in a hotel when she came to visit. The fact that he'd never introduced her to any of his friends or business colleagues. And since his death she had looked for his money, yet hadn't been able to find it.

It was hard for her to think of Reed as a criminal. He was her brother, first, last, and always, and she had loved him. And he had loved her. She couldn't ever doubt that.

She couldn't allow herself to cry over something that was beyond her control, not anymore.

Her life had just exploded around her, and she was in pieces, but it didn't matter.

Life went on and she had to cope with the pieces that remained.

She even had to cope with the fact that last night she had told Steven she loved him.

"Come on over," she said curtly when Steven answered his door. "Let's start looking."

She turned her back on him and hurriedly returned to Reed's apartment. After closing and locking his door, Steven followed her. "You've made the right decision, Kendall."

She turned on him, tension in every line of her body. "Save it. You made it clear I really didn't have a decision. I'm fed up with this mess and I just want it over with. I want you out of my life and I want to go home. So what are we looking for? How do we find it?"

He'd expected her anger and he could deal with it. What he was having a great deal of trouble dealing with was how completely she had withdrawn from him. She was a hundred and eighty degrees from the way she had been. She'd taken herself out of his reach and he was finding it very hard to bear.

"We're looking for something in this apartment that's worth ten million dollars."

She folded her arms and gazed around

her. "It's difficult for me to believe that there's something worth that much money here."

"Nevertheless we're fairly certain it's here. And whatever it is, it's what you and I have to find. We've already searched the place, of course, and—"

"And you had another opportunity to look at things when you were—quote, unquote—*helping* me." She sent him a look strong enough to wither plants on a vine.

But he simply nodded. "I was double-checking, but I didn't find anything. Whatever Reed did with the money, he was damned clever about it. If the Whartons hadn't caught on and Alden hadn't taken out after him that night, Reed would be safely in South America right now with his stolen fortune intact."

"I wish he was," she murmured.

"I'm sorry," he said immediately. "That was tactless of me."

"But it was the truth," she said dully. "Okay, let's concentrate. What about the art?" She waved her hand toward the walls. "I'm sure it's good stuff."

"It is, but the highest-valued piece is worth only fifteen thousand dollars."

"What about the value of all the pieces together?"

"Less than fifty thousand."

"That's what we can see," she said, still studying the art that hung around the room. "What about the possibility of a painting that was painted over the original? Or one canvas on top of an another, the bottom one being the one of value?"

"No. We've checked that all out."

She threw up her hands in frustration. "Then why in the hell do you think I can help if you've obviously gone over everything with a fine-tooth comb and haven't found anything?"

"Because you knew Reed better than any of us."

"Apparently not well enough," she said, bitterness scoring her tone.

"I'm talking about knowing him better personally. More than anyone else you knew his personal likes and dislikes. You knew if he liked peanut-butter-and-jelly sandwiches or—"

"He didn't. If there's a peanut-butter jar in his pantry, you'd better check it out. It might be filled with diamonds."

He countered her sarcasm with patience and composure. She had a right, he figured. "There's no peanut butter in his pantry. I was simply using that as an example."

"But you *do* know whether or not he had any, which makes my point. You haven't left any stone unturned. I don't know what else I can do."

"You can look at things with a fresh eye. Hopefully you'll see something no one else has."

She exhaled slowly. She was doing her best to hold herself together, to keep her hurt and anger contained, but it was an enormous task. Even being in the same room with Steven was painful. She'd see him pick up something or make a gesture and remember how his hands had felt on her body. She'd hear him say something and find herself looking at his lips, remembering how they had created fire on her skin. "I don't feel so fresh, Steven. I feel battered and tired. I don't think I can do this."

"If you want to go back to the normalcy of your life, you're going to have to."

She looked at him and again saw that hard implacability in his eyes. "Didn't you say you'd gathered information for an indictment for the Whartons? How many damned nails do you have to have for their coffin?"

"One more."

"I don't think you're going to get it."

"Yes, I am, and you're going to help me. Look, a few weeks ago I was ready to say we had all we could get on them. Basically I just wanted out. Then the Whartons found out about the ten million and Reed died. They told me to go to San Luis Obispo and check you out. Even though I was ready to wind everything down and get out, I went. That's when I saw you."

"You saw me because you were *spying* on me. Did you honestly think I was a criminal too?"

"The Whartons felt there was a possibility you knew about what was going on because of the letter Reed had started to write you."

She looked at him blankly. "Letter?"

"The one on his desk he left half-finished."

"The one where he said to remember that he wanted me to move down to South America and live with him?"

A small ironic smile touched his lips. "He said, *remember what I told you. It's important.* We had no idea what he was referring to. As far as the Whartons were concerned there was an excellent chance he told you what he'd done with the money. After all, you were his only living relative."

"And so you spied on me and broke into my house and went through my things."

"Yes." He gave her a long, measuring look, then spoke softly. "I'd say I was sorry again, but you don't want to hear it."

"No, I don't."

"And you don't want to hear me saying I was only doing my job."

"No, I don't."

His lips compressed into a straight line. "Is there anything I can say that would make it better?"

"Nothing." She brought her hands together in a show of determination. It was a fraudulent show. "Okay, where else could the money be?" Her gaze lighted on the large packing box of record albums that Reed had begun to pack. "Have you investigated these albums? They're rhythm-and-blues albums from the fifties. Reed once told me they were worth quite a bit of money."

"He was right. The collection is worth around twenty thousand dollars. When this is over I'll give you the name of a record collector who will help you sell them."

"Thanks, but no thanks. I don't want any proceeds from anything Reed bought with money made illegally."

"I can understand your feeling that way to a certain point, but if I were you I wouldn't let myself get too carried away with what is ethical and what is not ethical."

"Of course you wouldn't."

Once again he ignored her sarcasm. "I'm only thinking of you, Kendall. His life insurance might have been paid for with dirty money—I really don't know—but the proceeds of the policy come from the life-insurance company and are rightfully yours. Life is not all black and white. There's a lot of gray."

"I've always hated the color gray," she murmured, still staring at the records. It was much easier than looking at him. It seemed her heart broke a little more each time she did. "Have you checked inside the album covers? There might be something stuffed inside." Her tone turned facetious. "Or maybe one of the album covers is actually a priceless work of art."

"There's nothing inside them, and all the album covers are made out of cardboard with the artwork coming from photographs."

"Did you look at the labels? Maybe there's a state secret embedded somehow on one of them."

"You've been reading too many spy novels, Kendall."

"Not enough, I'd say." She folded her arms beneath her breasts. "Besides, I think this situation falls under the category of stranger-than-fiction."

Sympathy glinted in his eyes. "Only to you, because you've never been exposed to anything like it before. Your life is made up of children and fun evenings with your friends. You do your grocery shopping every Thursday night and go to the bank on Fri-

day. On the weekends you go to flea markets
to hunt for odd bits and pieces of things for
your art projects and occasionally find a special treat for the kids in your class."

She had trouble keeping her mouth from
falling open. "Just when I thought you
couldn't astound me anymore you go and do
it again. I'm surprised you haven't had me
X-rayed so that you could see clear through
me, but then I've been so open with you, you
really didn't have to do that, did you?"

He flinched. "You were very open right
from the first. That's why I knew you
weren't involved."

"How could you be so sure? I might have
been a wonderful actor, like you."

"You weren't and aren't," he said. He'd
always known right where he stood with her.
She had been so honest and free, she'd taken
his breath away.

"What else do you know about me?"

"I know that the computer salesman you
date occasionally isn't good enough for you."

"He's a very nice man."

"He's not for you."

"*I'll* be the one to decide that. Besides, I
at least know what his real job is."

"You also know what mine is now."

"Yes, now. Finally. And there's something
else I know—whatever happened between us,
you were only using me."

Anguish shot through him. He needed to keep them both focused on the job at hand, but he couldn't stand to hear her say that without trying to correct her. "No, that's not completely true."

"Oh, *please*, give me a break. You might have fooled me yesterday, but you're not going to fool me today."

"I wasn't using you when I made love to you, Kendall. I did it because I wanted to more than I've ever wanted anything else."

"I don't believe you."

"Believe it."

"You've lied to me about everything."

"Last night wasn't a lie."

"Last night was nothing more than a roll in the hay to you with someone who had been throwing herself at you right from the start. I didn't even know who you were!"

His eyes glittered with emotion. "Maybe you didn't know what I did for a living or why I was living next door to you, but you knew what I was feeling for you was as real as it gets. You *had* to know that."

With a vehement shake of her head she negated everything he had said. "*No*. I thought I did, but it turned out I was wrong."

He grabbed her arms and lightly shook her. "God, Kendall, don't you know that I was completely involved in what happened last night." The force of his emotions left his voice ragged and uneven. "That wasn't an FBI agent making love to you. It was *me*! No matter what I do for a living, I'm a *man* and I've wanted you since the first moment I laid eyes on you." He released her, but didn't step away, and his eyes glinted like heated lights. "You were out on the school playground and there were a dozen kids around you. You were laughing and you swept a little girl up in your arms and hugged her. I thought you were the most beautiful woman I'd ever seen. I still think that."

"*Stop* it! I can't bear to hear anymore!" She threw the words at him as if she were throwing daggers, but she was the one who was feeling the pain.

He couldn't hold back his agony any longer. "Kendall—" The doorbell rang. "Dammit!"

She expelled a pent-up breath. She didn't know what he was about to say, but she was extremely grateful for the interruption. If he'd told her one more time that last night had been real to him, she might have begun to soften toward him, and softening was the last thing she wanted or needed.

She started for the door, but Steven's hand snaked out and circled her upper arm, stopping her before she could get there. "What—"

He held his finger up to his lips. "Shh-hhh." He walked quietly to the door and glanced through the peephole, then came back to her, his expression grim. "It's Alden. He's probably here to see if he can jar or scare you into remembering where the money is."

"But I don't know where it is," she whispered back.

"*I* know you don't, but Alden is another matter."

"Then let's be quiet and maybe he'll think we're not here."

"He *knows* we're here. He's had us watched for days. Let him in and then follow my lead. Speak only if it's necessary, and above all be very, very careful."

TEN

When Kendall opened the door and saw Alden, her blood went cold. He was, she sensed instantly, a very dangerous man. She had to fight the urge to run and hide.

He gave her an easy smile as he strolled in. "Hello, Kendall. I'm Alden Wharton. I was a business colleague of your brother's." His gaze found Steven. "How nice to find you here too." He glanced back at her. "Steven is also a business colleague of mine."

He thought he was imparting information she didn't know, she realized, and kept quiet. He was worse than dangerous, she decided. He was deadly. His blond good looks and charming smile couldn't hide his menace. It seemed to ooze from his skin and permeate everything around him.

"What can we do for you today?" Steven

asked, casually moving forward. "I don't suppose you just happened to be in the neighborhood."

Ignoring Steven, Alden held out his hand to Kendall. "I thought it was about time Kendall and I met."

Unable to bear to have him touch her, she pretended she didn't see his hand and moved around him until Steven was between them. Alden's eyes narrowed, but he didn't comment.

Steven slipped his hands into his slacks pocket. "Why would you think that?"

"Because you're taking too long," Alden said, without bothering to hide his dislike for Steven.

Steven shrugged, the nonchalant gesture indicating better than words that he didn't care what Alden thought. "I disagree, and Kendall and I are busy right now. We're going through Reed's things, so if that's all . . . ?"

"Not by a long shot. Kendall and I have a lot to talk about. I have some information I think she'll be most interested to hear." The last was said as a taunt to Steven. Alden turned to her. "You may not know it, but you and I have been in an intimate situation before. I was the man who woke you up last night."

Fear had closed her throat, making it a

great effort to speak. "I know. I recognize your voice."

One eyebrow arched, the only sign he gave that he was surprised. "Do you also know I phoned you?"

"Yes. I told you to get a life. Have you?" She regretted the words the second she said them.

His smile sent chills through her, as he meant it to. "You know, you're very beautiful. It would be fun to get to know you better."

"As I said before," Steven drawled, "Kendall is very busy. We're *both* busy."

"Stay out of this, Steven."

"No way." He spoke softly but firmly. "I'm in it because Marcus wants me to be."

To Kendall's horror, Alden's features suddenly began to change. His eyes turned cold and his thin veneer of charm vanished, to be replaced by cruelty and hate and a frightening gleam of instability. Unconsciously she stepped closer to Steven.

"I bet she'd just love to know that you've only been spending time with her because you're working for us and we want our money back." He glanced at Kendall. "You didn't know that about loverboy, did you?"

"She knows," Steven said calmly. "I told her."

Alden lashed out with a quick fury. "You

son of a bitch! You went against a direct order from my father. You weren't supposed to tell her anything."

"If I went against the order, it was because I thought it best and because telling her would help us. I'm sure Marcus will understand. Especially when I tell him you must have come to the same conclusion, because you told her too. Or were you simply trying to make my job more difficult?"

Alden had the eyes of a stone-cold killer, Kendall thought. He'd kill them and then afterward go out to dinner and have a pleasant evening. Sweat trickled down her spine, but if Steven was sweating, it had to be ice water. He appeared composed and completely in control, his attention totally focused on Alden. But she was equally certain he knew every breath she drew.

"I'll give you two more hours," Alden said in a snarl.

A slightly amused smile crossed Steven's face. "And then what? I gather you have another plan to find the money?"

Alden's gaze cut to Kendall. "I can convince her to tell me where the money is. It'll be easy and we can get to know each other all at the same time. By the time it's all over, we'll be very close."

A shiver she couldn't suppress shuddered through her.

"Let me guess," Steven said pleasantly. "You're going to beat it out of her. What a great plan. You'll beat her senseless in hopes that she'll tell you something she never knew in the first place. How logical."

"You're a lousy bastard, Steven! It *is* logical. In fact it seems perfectly logical to me to kill you now. Then once she tells me where the money is, I'll get rid of her and take the money to my father."

Steven looked over at Kendall and smiled. "Alden believes that a dead person is a person who won't give you any trouble. What he tends to forget is that a dead person also won't give you any help."

He'd been handling Alden for two years, Kendall realized with a shock. It must have been something like mastering the art of muzzling a vicious dog. Or rendering a venomous snake helpless before it could bite you. Yet here Steven was, making it look almost easy when he had to know that Alden was a half inch away from killing him.

Alden unbuttoned his jacket and shifted his stance so that the gun tucked into his waistband was in clear view. He didn't reach for the gun, but just the sight of it scared Kendall to death.

"I don't care what my father says, you're not going to get much more time."

"I respect that, Alden," Steven said almost gently, "and I understand your need to hurry things along. In fact I'll call your father and tell him that very thing. It'll reassure him, don't you think?"

"You don't understand a damned thing, and as for my father, he made a big mistake when he put you in charge of this deal, and one way or another I'm going to prove it to him."

"Maybe he put me in charge because he saw how impetuous you were in going after Reed. If you hadn't been, things would have been a lot different. Marcus would have had his money and Reed would be alive. You want to impress your father? Then start thinking before you act." His words might be harsh, but he spoke them gently, calmly, pleasantly.

All the color drained from Alden's face, then rushed back, a splotchy red. Watching him, Kendall braced herself, sure he was about to snap.

But Steven kept talking to him in that calm, reasoning tone. "Your father understands that Kendall can't help us if she's too terrified to even think. As a matter of fact, I spoke with him just a few minutes ago. He was very happy when I told him that we're making progress."

Steven's glaring lies didn't faze Kendall as they once might have. He was facing down a maniac and somehow he was keeping control.

He strolled casually to the front door and opened it "It was nice seeing you. I'll call Marcus back and tell him you dropped by."

Alden's teeth came together with a snap. "*I'll* tell him. I'll also tell him that I've given you only twenty-four more hours."

Steven accepted the extra twenty-two hours with good grace and no show of having won a very important point. "Very well—have it your way. I'll notify you as soon as we find anything. See you later."

The gun still very much in evidence, Alden walked slowly past Steven and out of the apartment.

As soon as Steven closed the door, Kendall sank onto the couch with a loud sigh. "I've never been more afraid in my life. I thought he was going to kill us or at the very least you."

Without saying a word, he leaned back against the door and closed his eyes.

She gazed at him. The toll that controlling Alden had taken on him was clear to see. And he'd been doing it for two years, long before she'd arrived on the scene. "You were amazing," she said softly. "You're the one who kept him from doing anything worse than threatening us." She paused, but he still didn't say anything. "Are you all right?"

He pushed himself away from the door and took a seat in the armchair. "I'm fine. I'm sorry you had to be subjected to that scene, though."

"Thank God you were here."

He simply nodded. "He got to you twice and that's two times too many. I'm sorry."

"You said that."

"I mean it."

She fell silent for a moment, thinking about what had just happened and how he had reacted. "You've been living on a knife's edge the past two years, haven't you?"

For the first time since Alden had arrived, he looked directly at her. "Yes."

"You make it look relatively easy."

"It's never easy. In fact, the moment you let yourself think it's easy, the next moment you'll be dead."

"I can see that. He's not stable. What is his father thinking, letting him interfere with your assignment?"

He almost smiled at her indignation. "First of all, Marcus doesn't know anything about what Alden is doing except what I've told him. I told him about your being mugged. I didn't know about the phone call. I also didn't know Alden was going to sneak into your apartment until it happened, and . . . well, after that, things changed.

We spent the night together and then I told you everything this morning."

He said they spent the night together in the same tone he might use to describe a children's slumber party. But it had been far from an innocent night. It had been a night of fire and passion the likes of which she'd never experienced before. Everything had been so right. And now he was referring to it as if he'd already forgotten most of it.

"Next," he said, continuing, "you have to keep in mind that even though Marcus is of sound mind and likes to do business with as little mess and fuss as possible, he's also operating at all times outside the law. True, he can control Alden more than anyone else, but only to a certain extent, because basically Alden is a bomb waiting to explode."

"And when he explodes, his father is going to do what exactly?"

"Pick up the pieces and put him back together again with as little mess and fuss as possible, and go right on about his business."

She shook her head in astonishment. "Incredible. It's hard for me to believe that you've actually lived in that kind of world for so long."

A sad grin tugged at his lips. "I've lived in other worlds exactly like the Whartons' for longer than that. Besides, since when do you find it so hard to believe? Before Alden showed up, you were believing pretty much everything bad about me."

"That's because you told me it was true."

The grin vanished, but the sadness remained. "It is true. All of it. All of it except your belief that what I felt last night wasn't true. There's no way I could have faked that. I wouldn't have made love to you if I could have helped myself. And the simple truth is I *couldn't*. You'd tempted me for far too long."

"So you're saying it's my fault?"

Disappointed that she hadn't understood, he closed his eyes and rubbed the back of his lids. After a moment he looked at her again. "Nothing is your fault, Kendall. Everything is my fault."

She wished for her words back. They'd been accusatory when she'd really asked the question to get reassurance. And she was surprised that she needed it, but then the scene she'd just witnessed between him and Alden had shocked her into realizing what he'd been trying to tell her—that living a masquerade was the only way he'd been able to stay alive all this time.

She'd been able to see for herself how carefully he had to handle Alden, and volatile though he was, Alden was just one man in the Wharton organization. Steven would have had to deal with not only Marcus but everyone else, men like Alden, who craved power and approval. And through it all, Steven had protected her.

She wanted to say something to him, to convey what she was feeling. But when she tried to think of the words, she couldn't. She simply wasn't sure of anything anymore—right, wrong, what she wanted, what she didn't want. And there had already been so many words between them.

"Can I get you something to drink?" she finally asked.

"That would be nice."

Glad for the opportunity to do something, she rose and crossed to the wine shelves. "What would you like?"

"Why don't you open a bottle of Reed's wine? I think we both deserve a glass or two."

She certainly wasn't going to argue with him on that point, she thought, perusing the different bottles. As she'd said before, she knew nothing about wine, but she instinctively reached for one of the bottles she guessed was the least expensive. She definitely wanted something to drink, but she couldn't bring herself to open one of the more expensive kinds of wine. She wouldn't be able to enjoy it, knowing how Reed had gotten the money. "This one looks pretty good to me," she said, studying the label.

"It's a red wine and . . ." Her voice trailed off and she began to frown.

"What is it? Do you want me to open it?"

She looked at him, her forehead pleated with thought. "There are three bottles here that Reed had standing up, which implies that they're less expensive than the others, because Reed would never let a fine bottle of wine remain upright. He simply wouldn't be able to do it."

"So?"

"So—I never knew Reed to buy cheap wine. Even when he couldn't really afford the best, he'd save up for it."

All his senses alert, he surged to his feet and crossed to her. He took the bottle from her and studied the label and the bottle. Then he studied the next two bottles. "I can't really tell," he murmured. "Let's look at these in the sunlight." At the window he held up the bottles, one after the other, against the light. "There's something in this one," he said, holding the last bottle. "It's very hard to see because the glass is dark green and the wine is dark red, but I can just make out a shadow of something floating in there."

"Do you think Reed hid something in there?"

He tilted the bottle so that he could look

at the cork. "He could have. Didn't you say that he once bottled his own wine? That means he'd know how to seat a cork and seal it. Or he'd know someone who could. Also . . ."

"What?"

"I can't be sure—the bottle would have to be examined closer—but it looks as if the bottle was cut and resealed."

"How could he do that?"

"There are ways." He glanced at her. "He was very clever. He could have carried this wine on a plane in a carry-on bag and no one would have been the wiser. I'm going to have to break the bottle to get whatever is in it, but the worst thing that can happen is that I waste a cheap bottle of wine. Right?"

She nodded, even though she wasn't sure she agreed with him about the worst thing that could happen. If Reed had indeed hidden something inside the bottle, it would be proof positive that he had been a thief. And even though she knew in her heart that Steven hadn't lied to her about Reed, seeing the absolute proof was still going to hurt her.

She hadn't been prepared for just how much, she realized as a minute later she watched Steven pull a rolled canvas out of a sealed, acid- and waterproof container. When he unrolled the canvas and took away the special cloth it had been carefully rolled with, there could be no doubt as to what she was looking at.

A small oil, unmistakably a Picasso.

She gasped. "It was stolen, wasn't it?"

"He wouldn't have been able to buy it from a reputable dealer. That big a sale would have made the news."

"That's what I thought." Wrapping her arms around herself, she turned her back on the painting and returned to the couch.

Steven followed her. "Are you all right?"

"Sure." She gave a small, humorless laugh. "My adored brother not only stole ten million dollars from a crime family for which he was already performing illegal deeds, he laundered the money by buying a stolen painting. That makes it crime upon crime upon crime. But then I guess after the first crime it doesn't really matter, does it?"

He grimaced. "I wish there was something I could say to you that would make you feel better."

"I'm sure I'll work my feelings out about Reed eventually. I'll always love him. As you said he was clever, but I just wish he'd been clever enough to find a legitimate job. Or barring that, I wish he'd confided in me so that I could have had the chance to talk him out of what he was doing."

"Did you have that much influence with him?"

"I guess I'll never know."

"Maybe he knew you could talk him out of it and that's why he never told you."

"Like I said, I'll never know. He never gave me the opportunity." She shrugged and wished she could shrug Reed's actions away as easily. "You know, it was so like Reed to put his money into a Picasso. Under ordinary circumstances, he would never have been able to own such a painting. But it must have given him a real rush to know that for a little while he was the owner of a Picasso." Her laugh couldn't hide her pain. "Too bad he had to die for it."

"Yeah, it was."

She made an effort to pull herself together. "So what now?"

His gaze sharpened. "Now it's almost over. I'll contact McMurphy and then make arrangements for the transfer of the painting to the Whartons."

"You finally have that last nail for their coffin. You should be very happy."

"I should be," he agreed, gazing steadily at her.

"But you're not?"

"How can I be when you've been so hurt?"

"Doesn't that sort of thing come with the job description?" She waved off his comment as if it didn't matter, but it did. She knew it and so did he.

He started to say something, but then stopped himself. "I guess it's time for me to make those calls."

For the next hour Kendall sat quietly and watched and listened as Steven talked with both McMurphy and Marcus Wharton. It was another lesson for her in how skilled Steven was in walking a tightrope.

At last he hung up the phone and rubbed his face tiredly. "It's all set."

"What are the final plans?"

"We're going to take the twenty-four hours Alden gave us to make sure you'll be safe. The exchange will take place here and—"

"I heard you trying to persuade Marcus to come here. I wasn't sure you'd be able to do it."

"Basically it all came down to how badly he wanted his money back. Ten million is a great deal of money for anyone, even him. And I told him there was no way you'd come to them because Alden had scared the hell out of you. You'd only feel safe here."

"We won't be alone tomorrow when they come, will we?"

"No way. There'll be backup all around

us. That's why we're taking the extra time to make sure everyone and everything will be in place."

She exhaled slowly. "Thank goodness this is going to be over soon."

Yeah, he thought. And then she'd be gone, just as he had always known she would be. He rose from the dining table, where he'd been using the phone, and strolled into the living area, where she was. "You can go back to your normal life without fear."

And without him. She folded her hands together in her lap and looked down at them. "That'll be good. And I guess you'll be able to go on to your next assignment." She chanced a glance up at him and saw him gazing at her, an unreadable expression in his eyes. When he didn't speak, she went on. "Where do you really live?"

"I have a place not too far from here actually."

"I see." She felt awkward. She also felt a tremendous letdown. She'd known him only a short time, but since she'd met him he had filled her days and nights with his presence. After tomorrow, though, he would no longer be in her life. And she didn't have to wait until tomorrow to know that her life would seem very empty.

"The Bureau will be sending people over this evening to start setting up, but in the meantime I could help you sort through the rest of Reed's things, if you like."

She shook her head. "No."

A muscle in his jaw clenched. "I guess it's too much of a reminder of the time I spent lying to you."

There were a lot of reasons for her reluctance to let him help her—some she couldn't even name—so she simply said, "I've done enough sorting. There's very little I want—a table, a few personal things of Reed's. When I leave tomorrow I'll call the Salvation Army to come clear out the apartment. They can get a key from the building manager."

"So you're just going to walk away from it all?"

"It's really the best thing to do."

"I suppose. It's just that I didn't think you'd be leaving so soon."

"I can't think of any reason I should stay." She looked at him. "Can you?"

"You have to do what's best for you," he said, his voice flat and emotionless.

"That's what I thought." The silence stretched between them, working on her nerves. She had an incredible urge to cry. She felt as if there was a huge hole right through the middle of her and she didn't know how to begin to fix it. She rose. "Excuse me. I'm going to start packing."

She went to brush past him, but she had

only taken two steps when he grabbed her arm. "Kendall . . ." No longer emotionless, his voice was filled with pain and hunger. "God, don't go."

She stared up at him, her pulse racing. "Go where? You mean to pack?"

"Anywhere," he said, his tone almost desperate. "Dammit, don't go anywhere!"

"I—I'm not sure I understand." She'd given to him and then given some more. Then she had found out he had deceived her. She might be a little sadder now, a little wiser, but she was still the same person she had been last night when they had made love. And her body was responding to him every bit as much.

With a sound of self-disgust he abruptly let her go. "Never mind."

She reached out and placed her hand on his chest. A minute ago she wouldn't have believed herself capable of the action. But a minute ago she hadn't heard the desperation in his voice or seen the anguish etched on his face. Beneath her palm his heart pounded in double time. "What is it?" she asked softly.

With a muffled groan, he pulled her against him. "It's *hell*," he muttered. "It's flat-out hell." And he brought his mouth down hard on hers.

The thought of resisting flashed through her mind, but then desire flooded through her, desire that was hot, deep, and all-consuming. She'd regret this later, she thought hazily. But for now she wanted him with everything that was in her.

And he wanted her. She could feel the proof of his need for her straining against her. He trailed kisses all over her face and down her neck, then back up to her lips, where his tongue plunged wildly into the depths of her mouth. His hands roamed freely and possessively over her body to her breasts, to her hips, to her bottom, then back up to her breasts again.

He was barely controlled, barely tame. She could feel him trembling against her, feel the shudders of need as they racked through him. And she saw no reason to wait.

She reached for the waistband of his slacks and fumbled for how to undo it. A rough, desperate sound rumbled up from his chest and he swept her into his arms and carried her into the bedroom and to the bed. They were a tangle of arms and legs and clothes, but soon the clothes disappeared and they were left naked and entwined. And then he was thrusting into her. She heard herself cry out as pleasure shimmered through her, felt herself arch up to him, but nothing was conscious or intentional. Her response to him was beyond her control.

She heard him talking to her, but had no

idea what he was saying. Her body was in the grips of an ecstasy so strong, so hot, there was nothing or no one who could break through it. Time after time he drove into her until at last her climax came, shatteringly, powerfully.

Kendall stirred slowly awake. The drapes were drawn in the bedroom, blocking the daylight, and she had no idea what time it was. Without moving, she tried to look for a clock.

"It's about three-thirty in the afternoon."

She hadn't needed to hear Steven's voice to know that he was lying behind her in bed; she could feel the heat of his body.

"We'd better get dressed."

"We've got time before the guys show up." He came up on his elbow and with a gentle pressure to her shoulder rolled her over on her back so that he could look in her eyes. "First we have some things to talk about."

"What?" she asked cautiously.

"Last night when we were making love, you said you loved me. Did you mean it?"

She sat upright and grabbed the sheet to cover her. Physically she had wanted him and so she had made love with him one more time, one *last* time, but it had been an impulsive act she now regretted.

Emotionally she was completely spent. She simply wasn't up to one more confrontation. "There's no need to rehash this. We just had sex again. Okay, so fine. We're both consenting adults and we both obviously wanted it. No harm, no foul." She tried to get off the bed and at the same time bring the sheet with her. She had no desire to walk around nude.

He caught her arm. "You've closed up on me again, Kendall. Why?"

"Because you obviously want some sort of declaration from me and I have no intention of giving it to you."

"I asked a simple question. You said you loved me. Did you mean it?"

"I don't say things I don't mean."

The implication was there. *Unlike him*, she didn't say things that weren't true. But she'd still given him the answer he wanted. "Okay," he said gently, "let's just stop right here and take a deep breath. We're getting off the track."

"And the track is?"

"Kendall, I did a lot of things wrong, but I love you and that's the truth. That's why I asked whether or not you meant what you said."

"Why? If I'd said no, you wouldn't have told me?"

"No." He groaned. "I guess I did it all wrong, but I don't want you to leave tomorrow. Stay with me."

She stared at him. She must still love him because love simply didn't vanish overnight. On the other hand she couldn't *feel* the love anymore. Maybe it had been killed. "You're so good at playing a part. I bet even you get confused."

He sat up. "No. Not this time. Not with you."

"What makes this time different?"

"Because the Wharton case is over. I have no reason to lie to you anymore."

"Maybe you can't help yourself. You forget where one case lets off and a new one begins."

"You're wrong. I can't afford to forget. If I did, it could mean my life."

"And I can't allow myself to be fooled again."

He shifted around on the bed so that he was facing her. "I wouldn't. Not you, not ever again. Listen to me. I love you."

She shook her head. "I can't cope with your job, Steven. I'm not equipped to watch someone I love live lie after lie. Maybe that's the ultimate reason why Reed didn't tell me what he was doing. He knew me too well."

"I love you, Kendall. More than I ever thought possible."

At any time during the past week, before he had told her what was really going on, his words would have meant the world to her. But now . . .

"I made a mistake when I told you I love you." She spoke slowly, thinking as she went along. "Everything has happened too fast. I have to get away from you for awhile. I need time. I need peace and normalcy. I need to be able to think clearly."

He searched her face for several moments, but he found nothing in her expression to reassure him. "Then I guess I've got no choice but to let you go."

"That's right, you don't."

ELEVEN

The next day was foggy, which was entirely appropriate, Kendall reflected, as she stood quietly before Alden and Marcus. The fog provided the perfect backdrop for the secrecy, the lies, and deception that were playing out before her, along with yet another masquerade.

Steven was standing next to her and he was wired. Fully armed FBI agents were waiting in the next room. She'd been prompted to let Steven do most of the talking. Since Reed had laundered the money by buying the painting and there were no receipts, Steven had to get the Whartons to admit that the painting belonged to them, or some variation thereof.

She felt completely detached from what was happening. Nothing was touching her, not even the tension in the room. One way or another, everything would work out fine, and as soon as this final masquerade was over, she'd be on her way home. Her bags were already in her car downstairs. And she couldn't wait to leave.

She barely noticed the two men in front of her. They weren't important to her. But she couldn't help but watch Steven with a kind of aloof interest. He was handling Marcus and his son with his usual finesse. In fact, she appeared to be the last thing on his mind, which was fine with her. Since she'd known him, she had experienced a myriad of emotions, so many and so powerful she felt totally burned out. In fact she was sure there was nothing left inside her because she didn't seem capable of feeling anything.

"So where is it?" Alden snapped. "We're here. We want our money."

"Be patient," Marcus told his son in a congenial manner. "Steven wouldn't have invited us over if he didn't plan to give it to us."

Marcus was a distinguished-looking man with silver hair and patrician features. He looked like the president of a bank, Kendall reflected, who had a dozen grandchildren who came to visit him every Sunday. Instead he was the head of a very powerful crime family.

"Of course," Steven said, "but as Reed told you, it's no longer in money form. He did just as he said he did. He converted the money into something else worth ten million."

"Then give it to us," Alden said, his nerves obvious.

"Sure, but first I want to show it to you. You're really going to appreciate this, Marcus." Steven brought the canvas out from behind his back and held it up. "It's a Picasso. I did some checking and found out that it was stolen five years ago from a museum in France."

Marcus stepped closer to examine it, his eyes gleaming with admiration. "My God, it's a *masterpiece.*"

Alden shifted impatiently. "How do we know it's genuine? It might be a fake."

Marcus glanced at his son, then immediately returned his attention to the painting. "Reed wouldn't have put that sum of money into a fake. He would have gone to great lengths to verify it."

"I'm talking about Steven. He could have found the original and then substituted a copy."

"Steven wouldn't try to pass a fake off to us, because he knows that I will also go to great lengths to verify it."

Steven smiled. "Of course I do, and I can assure you it's the real thing."

Frustration crackled from Alden like electricity. "Even if it is genuine, you took way too long to find it. You were inefficient and sloppy, but I can guess why." His features twisted with jealousy, he shifted his gaze to Kendall. "All Steven's brains were below his belt, weren't they, sweetheart?"

She returned his gaze with equanimity. Because of Steven's explanation, she knew that Alden was trying to make Steven look bad in his father's eyes.

"Was she as good as she looks, Steven?"

"Alden! Don't be discourteous."

Marcus might order a person killed, Kendall reflected, but he would do it with wonderful manners.

"Oh, what the hell," Alden exclaimed with disgust. "Let's just get the damn painting and go."

Steven shook his head, his expression clearly conveying the fact that there was a problem that had him stumped. "There are no papers of ownership."

"Who the hell cares?" Alden practically shouted. "It's *ours.*"

"Really?" Steven said. "Are you sure?"

Marcus's head came up and his gaze narrowed with intensity on Steven, but before he could say or do anything, Alden burst out,

"Damn you, it was bought with money that belonged to us. That makes this painting ours."

With a smile Steven slowly handed it to Alden. "Then take it."

Agents burst in from the other room.

"You *fool*!" Alden shouted at Steven. "What have you done?"

"I believe he has set us up," Marcus said, his composure intact. Only his eyes showed a deadly fury.

Alden reached for the gun at his waistband, but before he could withdraw it Steven grabbed his arm and twisted it up behind his back. "Take it easy, Alden," he said, reaching around him and withdrawing the gun from his belt. "You've got nothing but time. Who knows? You may even learn to develop patience where you're going."

Kendall had taken a step back when the agents had burst into the room and now she watched untroubled as they went about their business with skill and efficiency.

And so it's over, she thought. So simple. So complicated. She had come to San Francisco an innocent—not that she'd known it—and now she'd never look at things in quite the same way again. Nor would her heart ever be whole again.

As soon as they hustled the Whartons

out, Steven came to her, his expression concerned. "Are you all right?"

"I'm fine." Nothing was reaching her, nothing was bothering her.

"I have to go into the office and wind this all up, but I should be able to break free by late afternoon. Wait for me. I want to talk with you."

"I'm going home. Now. Everything I said yesterday still goes. I need to get away from you. I need some peace to decide what's left in the world that's true."

He searched her face, his expression grim and sad. "I really did a number on you, didn't I?"

"Rest easy. It's not your fault. I left myself wide-open to you."

He took her chin between his thumb and forefinger and leaned down toward her. "And I fell in love with you. No matter what, don't forget that."

Kendall spent her first week back home completely numb and sleeping a lot. She didn't look at a clock or a newspaper or the television. She needed to heal, and instinctively she sought solitude and rest. She didn't want to think or feel or even talk.

The second week she emerged from her self-imposed isolation and made a half-hearted attempt to get back into her life, but she found that her life held no interest for her. When she was able to think or allowed herself to feel, she concentrated on trying to forget Steven's final words to her. She couldn't, though. Everything that had happened between them or that was said seemed permanently imprinted on her memory.

She tried to fill up her days by cleaning her house from top to bottom, but her house wasn't that big and her cleaning frenzy soon came to an end.

Unfortunately school was out for the summer and by the third week she badly needed something to do. Her feelings had come roaring back.

When nothing else worked to get her mind off Steven, she volunteered to help a friend run a recreation program for the kids at a local park. But that left her nights free, nights in which she lay in bed, remembering Steven. And aching for him.

One morning during her fourth week home, she walked out of the house to get the morning paper and saw him sitting in one of her porch rocking chairs.

Still half-groggy from sleep, she pushed her hair from her face. "What are you doing here?"

"Waiting for you. I got here about three this morning."

Her heartbeat had accelerated, she noticed absently, and all her senses had come to life. Her body was responding to him as if nothing had destroyed her belief in him and they hadn't ever been apart. "Three? Why didn't you ring the doorbell?"

"I didn't want to wake you. I thought I'd just wait. I didn't mind."

She stared at him, absorbing how wonderful he looked in tight-fitting, well-worn blue jeans paired with a matching sports jacket and a blue shirt open at the neck. She'd never seen him in jeans, and she had to admit that he looked sexier than she had ever seen him, and he was disconcerting her by seeming perfectly at home and comfortable in her wicker rocker. "What are you doing here?" she asked again.

He grinned ruefully. "I tried to stay away a little longer, but I couldn't. I waited as long as I could." He paused and his midnight-blue eyes grew even darker. "When you're all I can think about, the days and nights are very long."

She understood all too well. "I've thought about you too."

His ruefulness deepened. "I'd say it was a good sign, except I'm not sure it is." She didn't reply. "Not going to help me out here, are you?"

She hesitated, then gestured toward the

door. "Come in. I just brewed a fresh pot of coffee."

It was a start, he thought, following her into her house. It was definitely a start and he'd take it.

Her house was as he remembered it, warm, cozy, feminine. But most of all *she* was as he remembered. Golden, beautiful, sensual in her gold thigh-length silk robe and the white cotton T-shirt showing in the V of the robe's neckline.

He settled himself at her kitchen table and waited until she had served them both and taken the seat opposite him. "How have you been?" *Have you missed me?*

"Fine." *Missing you in spite of myself.*

"What have you been doing?" *Have you been dating that computer salesman?*

"I'm helping a friend at a recreational program." *I had to do something or I would have gone crazy thinking about you.*

"For kids?" *Is your friend male or female?*

"Don't you know?" *You were so good at finding out all about me before.*

"I'm out of the double-agent business." *Nothing matters without you.* He watched as she sipped at her coffee. "It was important work, Kendall, and I was very good at it."

"Yes, you were." *Sometimes I think it doesn't matter what you do for a living. I've missed you so much.*

"I did it for a long time, too long. Without even knowing it, I was burning out. But then I met you and I saw through your eyes what kind of life I was leading. Worse, I saw you get hurt and there wasn't a damned thing I could do to stop it. For that I will be eternally sorry."

"I hope you didn't come here to say another 'I'm sorry.'" *It's hard acting nonchalant when I can't stop looking at you.*

"No. I came to show you this." *I didn't think it was possible, but I love you more today than the day you left.*

He reached into his jacket pocket and withdrew a card. He placed it on the table and slid it across to her.

Without touching it she read it. STEVEN GANT, ATTORNEY-AT-LAW. "This is your business card—part of your cover story, right? So what? You can have five hundred run up at a local print shop for practically nothing."

"This is for real. I'm back to practicing corporate law as my brother's partner. Of course I'm going to have to burn a lot of midnight oil studying." He grinned. "Luckily Mitch constantly ran things by me, hoping to lure me back into the partnership."

"And I'm supposed to care?" *I care.*

"I hoped you would." *Please care.*

She got up, walked to the counter, and stood, staring out the window, her back to him. *If you are telling the truth, it would mean you will no longer be in danger and I won't have to worry about your safety as I have been in the loneliness of the night.*

He shifted in the chair so that his body was angled toward her. "You don't have to listen to me, but I've got to say this anyway." *Oh, God, please hear and understand what I'm saying.* "The advantage I always had in doing my job is that nothing or no one touched me. I was completely jaded. I had done it all and seen it all. And then *you* walked into my life. I took one look at you and I was down for the count."

What are you saying? Slowly she turned back around.

Encouraged by the action, he went on. "Oh, I had delusions that I could be objective about you and what I had to do, but those delusions bit the dust pretty damned quick. And I had to totally forget about control. All my skills that had stood me in such good stead on the job up to that point vanished." His voice dropped and gentled. "I looked at you, Kendall, and fell in love, hopelessly, completely."

I believe you. Suddenly she couldn't breathe. "Steven, I—"

"No, wait. You don't have to say a thing." *I'm so afraid that you'll tell me to leave.* "I didn't come here to put you on the spot. I only came here to say what I didn't get a chance to say before. I know that I have to live with the fact that nothing I can say or do is ever going to change what you feel or think about me."

You're right. No matter what, I'll always love you. She moved restlessly, realizing she had to face the fact that it hadn't really ended with the two of them. It had simply stopped for a period of time while she healed.

She had become overwhelmed by everything and everyone and had dealt with her problem by leaving. Now, even though she'd admitted to herself that she still loved him, she had doubts about the two of them. There was a chasm between them and she didn't know if it was possible to build a bridge. "So are you happy in the law firm with your brother?"

"I like the work." *I hate being without you.*

"If a man gives up something for a woman, he'll come to resent her." *I'd rather be apart from you than have you resent me the rest of our lives.*

"You think I quit because of you? No." He slowly shook his head. "You just opened my eyes. It was time for me to do something different. You can only walk on the tightrope for so long and then you've got to get off or you'll lose your balance and fall."

Could you possibly mean that? Have you thought it through? "Really?"

Please believe me. He took a piece of paper out of his inside jacket pocket and handed it to her. She unfolded it and scanned it, then looked at him.

"This is your resignation from the Bureau."

"Written the day after you left."

"Then you've had a few weeks to think about your decision and you're still certain you did the right thing?" *I have to be sure.*

"Absolutely. I have no regrets." *I only regret what happened to you.* "If I'd never met you, I would have still come to the same conclusion, but it might have been at some later date and the conclusion might have come too late. But I did meet you and the conclusion came sooner and it was just in time. There's not a doubt in my mind that it was the right decision for me to make."

So now it was her turn to make a decision, but was there really a decision to make? *I don't think I could face it if you went back to San Francisco without me.* "Remember when I told you I made a mistake in telling you I loved you?"

His lips twisted into a slight grin, but the expression in his eyes remained serious. "Yes." *How could I forget something like that?*

"I meant that I shouldn't have said it—

not that soon, not without knowing you better. For my sake I should have been more circumspect." *I should have guarded my heart more, but it seemed so right to give it to you.*

"I can't tell you how glad I am that you weren't." Equal portions of fear and hope were threatening to choke him and close his throat. "So . . ." *Even though you're saying you shouldn't have said it that soon, did you mean it?*

She started toward him. "I'm very glad to see you."

But do you love me? Hopeful, fearful, he held his arms out to her, but he didn't reach for her. It was her call, her decision. She stopped in front of him, but made no other move, and the next moments passed like hours.

Then she came down on his lap and slid her arm around his neck, all softness and golden femininity and perfumed skin. "I love you, Steven."

She kissed him and his heart swelled with a love so boundless he was overwhelmed by it. In years past there'd been days when he was sure his heart was no longer working, days when he'd been convinced he had no soul. But now Kendall was both his heart and soul. "I love you, and I'll never lie to you again," he murmured against her mouth. "And I'll never let you go."

EINSTEIN AND PINK
ARE HAVING A BABY!
IS IT A BOY OR A GIRL?
HOW WILL THE PROUD PARENTS CHOOSE
A NAME?
PLEASE, THEY NEED YOUR HELP!

- You first met Einstein, everybody's favorite artificial intelligence computer, in Ruth Owen's debut novel MELTDOWN, LOVESWEPT #558.

- In SMOOTH OPERATOR, LOVESWEPT #632, Einstein met his match in PINK—a computer who could really blow his fuse!

- But their true love was tested in SORCERER, LOVESWEPT #714, when PINK had to save Einstein from a microchip/intelligence/byte threatening virus.

- Now Einstein and PINK are expecting a baby. The only problem is, they need a name. . . .

Read the Official Rules to find out what you need to do to enter LOVESWEPT'S NAME THE BABY COMPUTER CONTEST.

Now, share in PINK and Einstein's excitement as they await their new arrival, and win a chance to give them the gift that will last a lifetime!

LOVESWEPT'S "NAME THE BABY COMPUTER" CONTEST
OFFICIAL RULES:

1. *No purchase is necessary.* Enter by printing or typing your name, address, and telephone number at the top of a piece of 8 1/2" × 11" plain white paper, if typed, or lined paper, if handwritten. Below your name and address, write the name (and gender) you're suggesting for Einstein's and PINK's baby, and an essay of no more than 100 words explaining what gave you the idea for the suggested name for the baby computer. If you need inspiration, Einstein was first introduced to LOVESWEPT readers in MELTDOWN by Ruth Owen, Einstein met PINK in Ruth Owen's SMOOTH OPERATOR, and their true love was tested in Ruth Owen's SORCERER. Each of these books is readily available in libraries. Once you've completed your entry form, mail your entry to: LOVESWEPT'S "NAME THE BABY COMPUTER" CONTEST, Dept. SS, Bantam Books, 1540 Broadway, New York, NY 10036.

2. PRIZES (3): *First Prize (1):* The name suggested by the First Prize winner will be the name used for Einstein's and PINK's baby in Ruth Owen's next LOVESWEPT novel (scheduled for publication in May 1996). The First Prize winner also will be profiled and pictured in the back of that book as well as in the back of the other May 1996 LOVESWEPTs and will receive autographed copies of each of Ruth Owen's LOVE-SWEPT novels involving Einstein and PINK. (Approximate retail value: $15.00.) *Second Prize (2):* The two Second Prize winners will receive autographed copies of the May 1996 Ruth Owen LOVESWEPT novel which introduces the baby computer and also will be named in the back of that book and the other May 1996 LOVESWEPTs as runners up to the First Prize winner. (Approximate retail value: $4.50.)

3. Contest entries must be postmarked and received by August 1, 1995, and all entrants must be 21 or older on the date of entry. The entries submitted will be judged by Ruth Owen and members of the LOVESWEPT Editorial Staff on the basis of the originality and creativity shown in the choice of a name for the baby computer and the thoughtfulness and writing ability reflected in the accompanying essay. If there are insufficient entries or if, in the judge's sole opinion, no entry contains a suitable name for the baby computer, Bantam reserves the right not to declare a winner for either or both Prizes. If Bantam determines not to award the First Prize, any winners selected for the Second Prize will receive an autographed copy of the May 1996 Ruth Owen LOVESWEPT which introduces the baby computer but will not be named in the back of that book and the other May 1996 LOVESWEPTs. All of the judges' decisions are final and binding. All essays must be original. Entries become the property of Bantam Books and will not be returned. Bantam Books is not responsible for incomplete or lost or misdirected entries.

4. Winners will be notified by mail on or about September 1, 1995. Winners have 14 days from the date of notice in which to accept their prize award or an alternate winner will be chosen. Odds of winning are dependent on the number of entries received. Prizes are non-transferable and no substitutions are allowed. Winners may be required to execute an Affidavit Of Eligibility And Promotional Release supplied by Bantam Books and the First Prize Winner will need to supply a photograph for inclusion in the one-page profile. Entering the Contest constitutes permission for use of the winner's name, address (city and state), photograph, biographical profile, and the name and essay submitted for publicity and promotional purposes, with no additional compensation.

5. Employees of Bantam Books, Bantam Doubleday Dell Publishing Group, Inc., their subsidiaries and affiliates, and their immediate family members are not eligible to enter. This Contest is open to residents of the U.S. and Canada, excluding the Province of Quebec, and is void wherever prohibited or restricted by law. Taxes, if any, are the winner's sole responsibility.

6. The winners of the Contest will be announced in Ruth Owen's May 1996 LOVE-SWEPT novel as well as in other LOVESWEPTs published in May 1996.

THE EDITORS' CORNER

Be sure to scope out a spot in the shade to share with the four sultry LOVESWEPT romances headed your way next month. This picnic packs a menu of intoxicating love stories spiced with passion and a hint of fate.

USA Today bestselling author Patricia Potter cooks up an intoxicating blend of conflict and emotions in her latest, **IMPETUOUS**, LOVESWEPT #746. Like an exotic gypsy, PR whiz Gillian Collins sweeps into Steven Morrow's office and begins her crusade to win his consent for a splashier grand opening of his latest project! He's always preferred practical, reliable, safe—but Gillian enchants him, makes him hunger for pleasures he's never known. Patricia Potter demonstrates how good it can be when the course of true love doesn't quite run smooth.

Judy Gill offers double doses of love and laughter with **TWICE THE TROUBLE**, LOVESWEPT #747. Maggie Adair is magnificent when riled, John Martin decides with admiration—no lioness could have protected her cub more fiercely! But once Maggie learns that her adopted daughter and his were twins separated at birth, shock turns to longing for this man who can make them a family, a lover who needs her fire. Judy Gill transforms a surprising act of fate into this witty, touching, and tenderly sensual romance.

The moment she sees the desert renegade, Carol Lawson instantly knows Cody Briggs is her **DREAM LOVER**, LOVESWEPT #748, by Adrienne Staff. Seeing the spectacular mesa country through his eyes awakens her senses, makes her yearn to taste forbidden fire on his lips—but when Cody offers to trade his secrets for hers, she runs. Mesmerizing in emotion, searing in sensuality, this spellbinding tale of yearning and heartbreak, ecstasy and betrayal, is Adrienne Staff's most unforgettable novel yet.

With more sizzle than a desert at high noon, Gayle Kasper presents **HERE COMES THE BRIDE**, LOVESWEPT #748. Nick Killian's underwear is as wicked as his grin, Fiona Ames thinks as the silk boxers spill all over the luggage carousel from his open suitcase! She's flown to Las Vegas to talk her father out of marrying Nick's aunt, never expecting to find an ally in the brash divorce lawyer. When the late-night strategy sessions inspire a whirlwind romance, Nick vows it won't last. Can Fiona show him their love is no mirage? Experience Gayle Kasper's special talent for creating delectable characters whose headlong fall into love is guaranteed to astonish and delight.

Happy reading!

With warmest wishes,

Beth de Guzman   Shauna Summers

Senior Editor   Associate Editor

P.S. Watch for these spectacular Bantam women's fiction titles slated for July: From *The New York Times* bestselling author Amanda Quick comes her newest hardcover, **MYSTIQUE**, a tantalizing tale of a legendary knight, a headstrong lady, and a daring quest for a mysterious crystal; fast-rising star Jane Feather spins a dazzling tale of espionage in **VIOLET** in which a beautiful bandit accepts a mission more dangerous than she knows; **MOTHER LOVE**, highly acclaimed Judith Henry Wall's provocative new novel, tests the limits of maternal bonds to uncover what happens when a child commits an act that goes against a mother's deepest beliefs; in Pamela Morsi's delightful **HEAVEN SENT**, the preacher's daughter sets out to trap herself a husband and ends up with the local moonshiner and a taste of passion more intoxicating than his corn liquor; Elizabeth Elliott's spectacular debut, **THE WARLORD,** is a magical and captivating tale of a woman who must dare to love the man she fears the most. Check out next month's LOVESWEPTS for a sneak peek at these compelling novels. And immediately following this page, look for a preview of the wonderful romances from Bantam that *are available now!*

Don't miss these extraordinary books
by your favorite Bantam authors

On sale in May:

FAIREST OF THEM ALL
by Teresa Medeiros

TEMPTING MORALITY
by Geralyn Dawson

"Ms. Medeiros's prolific imagination
will leave you spellbound."
—*Rendezvous*

FAIREST OF THEM ALL

by best-selling author
TERESA MEDEIROS

Teresa Medeiros has skyrocketed into the front ranks of best-selling romance authors following the phenomenal success of THIEF OF HEARTS, WHISPER OF ROSES, and ONCE AN ANGEL. FAIREST OF THEM ALL is her most enchanting romance ever.

She was rumored to be the fairest woman in all of England. But Holly de Chastel considered her beauty a curse. She had turned away scores of suitors with various ruses, both fair and foul. Now she was to be the prize in a tournament of eager knights. Holly had no intention of wedding any of them and concocted a plan to disguise her beauty. Yet she didn't plan on Sir Austyn of Gavenmore. The darkly handsome Welshman was looking for a plain bride and Holly seemed to fit the bill. When he learned that he'd been tricked, it was too late. Sir Austyn was already in love—and under the dark curse of Gavenmore.

Sweeter than the winds of heav'n is my lady's
    breath,
Her voice the melodious cooing of a dove.
Her teeth are snowy steeds,
Her lips sugared rose petals,
That coax from my heart promises of love.

Holly smothered a yawn into her hand as the minstrel strummed his lute and drew breath for another verse. She feared she'd nod off into her wine before he got around to praising any attributes below her neck. Which might be just as well.

A soulful chord vibrated in the air.

The envy of every swan is my lady's graceful
    throat,
Her ears the plush velvet of a rabbit's
Her raven curls a mink's delight.
But far more comely in my sight—

Holly cast the generous swell of her samite-clad bosom a nervous glance, wondering desperately if *teats* rhymed with *rabbit's*.

The minstrel cocked his head and sang, "are the plump, tempting pillows of her—"

"Holly Felicia Bernadette de Chastel!"

Holly winced as the minstrel's nimble fingers tangled in the lutestrings with a discordant twang. Even from a distance, her papa's bellow rattled the ewer of spiced wine on the wooden table. Elspeth, her nurse, shot her a panicked look before ducking so deep into the window embrasure that her nose nearly touched the tapestry she was stitching.

Furious footsteps stampeded up the winding stairs toward the solar. Holly lifted her goblet in a half-hearted toast to the paling bard. She'd never grown immune to her father's displeasure. She'd simply learned to hide its effects. As he stormed in, she consoled herself with the knowledge that he was utterly oblivious to the presence of the man reclining on the high-backed bench opposite her.

Bernard de Chastel's ruddy complexion betrayed the Saxon heritage he would have loved to deny. Holly's trepidation grew as she recognized the ducal seal on the wafer of wax being methodically kneaded by his beefy fist.

He waved the damning sheaf of lambskin at her. "Have you any idea what this is, girl?"

She popped a sweetmeat in her mouth and shook her head, blinking innocently. Brother Nathanael, her acerbic tutor, had taught her well. A lady should never speak with her mouth occupied by other than her tongue.

Flicking away the mangled seal with his thumb, her papa snapped open the letter and read, " 'It is with great regret and a laden heart that I must withdraw my suit for your daughter's hand. Although I find her charms unparalleled in my experience' "—he paused for a skeptical snort—" 'I cannot risk exposing my heir to the grave condition Lady Holly described in such vivid and disturbing detail during my last visit to Tewksbury.' " Her father glowered at her. "And just what condition might that be?"

"Webbed feet," she blurted out.

"Webbed feet?" he echoed, as if he couldn't possibly have heard her correctly.

She offered him a pained grin. "I told him the firstborn son of every de Chastel woman was born with webbed feet."

Elspeth gasped in horror. The minstrel frowned

thoughtfully. Holly could imagine him combing his brain for words to rhyme with *duck*. Her father wadded up the missive, flushing scarlet to the roots of his graying hair.

"Now, Papa, are you *that* eager to see me wed?"

"Aye, child, I am. Most girls your age are long wedded and bedded, with two or three babes at the hearth and another on the way. What are you waiting for, Holly? I've given you over a year to choose your mate. Yet you mock my patience just as you mock the blessing of beauty our good Lord gave you."

She rose from the bench, gathering the skirts of her brocaded cotehardie to sweep across the stone floor. "Blessing! 'Tis not a blessing, but a curse!" Contempt thickened her voice. " 'Holly, don't venture out in the sun. You'll taint your complexion.' 'Holly, don't forget your gloves lest you crack a fingernail.' 'Holly, don't laugh too loud. You'll strain your throat.' The men flock to Tewksbury to fawn and scrape over the musical timbre of my voice, yet no one listens to a word I'm saying. They praise the hue of my eyes, but never look *into* them. They see only my alabaster complexion!" She gave a strand of her hair an angry tug only to have it spring back into a flawless curl. "My raven tresses!" Framing her breasts in her hands, she hefted their generous weight. "My plump, tempting—" Remembering too late who she was addressing, she knotted her hands over her gold-linked girdle and inclined her head, blushing furiously.

The duke bowed his head, battling the pained bewilderment that still blamed Felicia for dying and leaving the precocious toddler to his care. Holly had passed directly from enchanting child with dimpled knees and tumbled curls to the willowy grace of a woman grown, suffering none of the gawkiness that so frequently plagued girls in their middle years.

Now she was rumored to be the fairest lady in all of England, all of Normandy, perhaps in all the world.

"I've arranged for a tournament," he said without preamble.

"A tournament?" she said lightly. "And what shall be the prize this time? A kerchief perfumed with my favorite scent? The chance to drink mulled wine from the toe of my shoe? A nightingale's song from my swan-like throat?"

"You. You're to be the prize."

Holly felt the roses in her cheeks wither and die. She gazed down into her father's careworn face, finding its gravity more distressing than anger. She towered over him by several inches, but the mantle of majesty he had worn to shield him from life's arrows since the death of his beloved wife added more than inches to his stature.

"But, Papa, I—"

"Silence!" He seemed to have lost all tolerance for her pleas. "I promised your mother on her deathbed that you would marry and marry you shall. Within the fortnight. If you've a quarrel with my judgment, you may retreat to a nunnery where they will teach you gratitude for the blessings God has bestowed upon you."

His bobbing gait was less sprightly than usual as he left Holly to contemplate the sentence he'd pronounced.

Dire heaviness weighted Holly's heart. *A nunnery.* Forbidding stone walls more unscalable than those that imprisoned her now. Not a retreat, but a dungeon where all of her unspoken dreams of rolling meadows and azure skies would rot to dust.

What are you waiting for, Holly? her papa had asked.

Her gaze was drawn west toward the impenetrable tangle of forest and craggy dark peaks of the Welsh mountains. A fragrant breath of spring swept through her, sharpening her nameless yearning. Genuine tears pricked her eyelids.

"Oh, Elspeth. What *am* I waiting for?"

As Elspeth stroked the crown of her head, Holly longed to sniffle and wail. But she could only cry as she'd been taught, each tear trickling like a flawless diamond down the burnished pearl of her cheek.

TEMPTING
MORALITY
by Geralyn Dawson

"One of the best new authors to come along in years—fresh, charming, and romantic!"*

She was a fraud. That's what Zach Burkett thought when he caught sight of Miss Morality Brown testifying at a town meeting. A deliciously enticing fraud would be the perfect cover for his scheme to pay back the "godly" folk of Cottonwood Creek for their cruel betrayal. But Zach was wrong: far from being a con, the nearly irresistible angel was a genuine innocent. And only after he'd shamelessly tempted her to passion would he discover that he'd endangered his own vengeful heart.

He was the answer to her prayers. That's what Morality Brown thought when she gazed up into Zach Burkett's wicked blue eyes. It hardly mattered that the slow-drawling, smooth-talking rogue was a self-confessed sinner, or that she sensed a hidden purpose behind his charm. In his arms, she found the heaven she'd always longed for. But all too soon, she'd discover the terrible truth about the man who'd stolen her heart. Scarred by the past, he lives for revenge—and it will take a miracle of love to save his soul.

* *New York Times* best-selling author Jill Barnett

Flickering torches cast shadows across the faces of the faithful gathered to hear Reverend J. P. Harrison, founder of the Church of the Word's Healing Faith, preach his message. Anticipation gripped the listeners as the reverend stepped up to the lectern, and the low-pitched murmur of voices died as he sounded out a greeting.

"Brothers and sisters in the Lord!" boomed J. P. Harrison. "I have travelled God's great southland long enough to learn that wherever a few of His children are gathered together, devil doubts and disbelief walk among us." Thick salt-and-pepper eyebrows lowered ominously when he stared into faces as if searching for signs of the devil.

His voice dropped. "Doubting Thomases lurk here even now, maybe sitting next to you." Silence descended on the crowd as individuals shot nervous glances to those seated at their sides.

"But the gospel truth . . ." the reverend's cry rang out. "The gospel truth is that God's work needs the support of Doubting Thomases, too! In a few moments, I'll tell you how each and every one of you assembled here tonight can lend a hand to the Lord's work. Right now, I want you to rejoice with me in God's Miracles."

With an actor's sense of timing, he waited, hands uplifted, for the swell of voices from the crowd to subside. Then he reached into the pulpit and pulled out a stack of newsprint. "*The Petersburg Republican, The Greenville Mountaineer, The Charleston Daily Courier*, all carry word of God's work on their front pages." Waving one of the papers, he roared, "I don't ask you to take my word for God's glory. Trust your own eyes, your own ears. Open your hearts to His greatness working among us."

The reverend pulled a pair of wire spectacles from his vest pocket and hooked them over his ears. Brandishing a news sheet, he read with reverence, " 'Miracle Miss Cured.' " Holding up a second paper, he intoned, " 'Miracle Worked Before Hundreds.' " Tone rising to full bellow, he cried, " 'Reverend Harrison Heals Blind Niece Before Charleston's Elite!' " He held the newspapers aloft while murmurs rippled through the assembly.

Dropping the sheets back onto the pulpit, the reverend spoke in a voice as soft as the night breeze. "But you, my brothers and sisters, *you* don't have to believe these fine newspapers. God's Miracle waits among us here in Cottonwood Creek, Texas, tonight. Open your hearts to proof of God's greatness, straight from one who personally knows His healing. Brothers and sisters, I give you my niece, Miss Morality Brown."

Zach sat up. He blinked his eyes, then looked again. My Lord, the gal could make a cowboy forget his horse.

The gray dress fit her like paper on the wall, displaying the kind of curves that made a man's mouth water. Yet, as bountiful as were her womanly gifts, the young lady who stood before the crowd was the very picture of wide-eyed innocence.

It was a nearly irresistible combination.

"Good evening." She folded her hands demurely and spoke in a strong, sincere voice. "I stand here before you to offer testimony of the miracle the Lord worked through the hands of my uncle, Reverend Harrison."

Zach's mouth lifted in a sardonic grin. Well, who'd have thought it? The gal was a hell of an actress. Lies and miracles, huh?

Everything was a scam.

"I was a young girl when an accident caused me to go blind," she declared. "For years I lived in a world of darkness, able to do little for myself, dependent upon others for the most simple things. I didn't even know my loved ones' faces. It was a sad and lonely existence, despite the efforts of my uncle and his wife, God rest her soul."

Keep tugging those heartstrings, sweet one, and their fingers will reach deeper into pockets.

Miss Brown glanced at him, and Zach lifted a brow at the nervousness she betrayed in that fleeting moment. She continued, "My uncle's work sent us from city to city, and in every one, my aunt would seek out the best doctors to examine my eyes. Time and again we were told to accept my condition as permanent. Following my aunt's untimely death, reality forced me to abandon hope of a cure."

She was good. Zach casually shifted in his seat to get a look at the folks sitting beside him. *Got 'em hooked, honey. Reel 'em in.*

Almost as if she'd heard him, she said, "Then, eight years ago in Charleston, West Virginia, a miracle happened. The day began as any other. My uncle set up his booth at a fair where he demonstrated the revolutionary new cleaning compound he had invented. I assisted as best I could, working mainly with a cotton cloth he used in the demonstrations. While I wasn't aware of it at the time, my uncle made it a practice to pray every day for my deliverance from affliction."

Pausing, she gifted the crowd with an angelic smile. "That spring morning, the Lord chose to answer his prayers."

Miss Brown reached for a cup atop a table behind

the pulpit, sipped at its contents, then returned it to its place. Zach nodded. Timing was right on the mark.

Her voice rang out on the cool night air. "I was sitting at a table, testing the texture of different squares of cloth and dividing them into stacks for my uncle's use. He visited with the city fathers a short distance away. I heard them conclude their conversation, and my uncle approached our booth." She shrugged her shoulders in an endearing, embarrassed manner and added, "He later told me he observed the mess I'd made of my task and silently asked the Lord to heal me."

Again Zach glanced nonchalantly over his shoulder. Many good folk were perched on the edge of their seats. By the looks of it, this hoax might work as well as any he'd seen during his days on the swindle circuit. He was impressed.

"The moments that followed are burned into my memory," Morality Brown declared with conviction. "I heard my uncle shout, 'God bless Morality.' He touched me, and from his hands, I felt a colossal force. It rocked me, an energy beyond description. Then, I saw a flash of brilliant, overpowering light, and I fainted."

She stopped and surveyed her audience, sincerity shining in round, moss-colored eyes. In a quiet voice filled with wonder and ringing with truth, she said, "And when I awoke, my sight had returned. I could see again."

"And now it's your turn to take part in God's marvelous works," Harrison declared. "Your hands, like mine, can be instruments of the Lord. I want every one of you to put a hand in his pocket or her purse. I want you to pull out the largest bill, the largest coin you have on you. I want your hands joined with mine in God's, to support the healing work the Lord Himself has empowered me to do."

The good people of Cottonwood Creek all but fell over themselves in their rush to add their contributions to the plate. Zach Burkett didn't bother to check the denomination of the coin he tossed in. He sat with his head cocked to one side, his gaze considering Morality Brown and the spectacle hosted by her uncle.

This gal was great, her uncle's show convincing. How the hell could he use them?

Zach pondered the problem, standing with the others as they lifted their voices in "Just As I Am." Halfway through the first verse, a speculative smile spread across his face like honey on a hot roll. His bass voice boomed, joining the multitude in song.

Zach Burkett had seen the light.

And don't miss these electrifying
romances from Bantam Books,
on sale in June:

From *New York Times* best-selling author
Amanda Quick comes

MYSTIQUE

Amanda Quick "taps into women's
romantic fantasies with a master's touch."
—Janelle Taylor

VIOLET

by best-selling author

Jane Feather

"An author to treasure."
—*Romantic Times*

MOTHER LOVE

by acclaimed author

Judith Henry Wall

"Wall keeps you turning the pages."
—*San Francisco Chronicle Review*

WARLORD

by up-and-coming author

Elizabeth Elliott